A
STORYTELLING
OF
RAVENS

R R PENFOLD

CRANTHORPE
MILLNER
PUBLISHERS

First published by Cranthorpe Millner Publishers (2024)

ISBN 978-1-80378-249-2 (Paperback)

www.cranthorpemillner.com

Cranthorpe Millner Publishers

Printed and bound by CPI Group (UK) Ltd
Croydon, CR0 4YY

MIX
Paper | Supporting responsible forestry
FSC
www.fsc.org
FSC® C013604

Prologue

'Twas a bleak November day in the year of our Lord 1863. A cold day. A dark, bitter, unrelenting and, some would say, Godless day. For sure there was no sign of his mercy. Instead, this was a time when the leaves had fled the trees to leave their branches black skeletons against grey sky, all life within them frozen and their purpose gone. On that dark day they stood motionless along the riverbank unless struck by icy wind coming off that same river, itself just as dark and bleak.

The mid-afternoon sun gave no heat and such little light that the far side of the river could barely be seen; its buildings no more than dark shadows against the grey, their form obscured by the winter gloom. Certainly this was no day for the God-fearing; no day for those who flinched at shadows or might wonder what they hid. They needed to be safely indoors with candles lit and fires burning.

That notwithstanding, many were about despite the cold for this was no country stream, no rural idyll. This was a main river, an industrial river, wide filthy and deep where it cut through the heart of the city. All fish gone, all life gone, its sole purpose now was to carry the boats taking goods to and from the inhuman factories which in their turn poisoned the river while giving the city its wealth, and also its purpose.

Important to be sure, but on that day the river had another purpose. A Godless, merciless purpose which the people along its banks knew full well. It was why they were there. On such occasions crowds would always be there, attracted as they were by tragedy.

"Went in off the bridge so they say," a figure announced to those who would listen.

"Jumped most likely," answered another at which heads nodded sagely.

"Not the only one either," an old crone told them as she clutched her coat tight against her thin body, seeking protection from the cold. "There's been a few of them just lately."

She looked at them, as they looked back at her, with naught else to say. Just recently that river had seen many fatalities, too many as some would have it. Now it seemed another had been added to that macabre list for the attraction of the crowd now assembled.

Somewhere, as it transpired, a tormented soul had thrown itself into the water and where his body now lay only the river knew. The secret hidden in its dark depths away from the sight of Man. Away from the sight of all living creatures, except one.

Perhaps by the grace of God there was one creature whose blessing, or whose curse, was to know. Why that should be only He who gave life to all could answer, yet know they did. They always had done. They always would. While other creatures remained dumb, senseless even, they would know, but only they.

Alone out of all other creatures in this mortal world they could see that which was hidden. Certainly, no river could hide anything from them when they came looking – and come they did. Flying in on black wings the ravens began to arrive.

Just one at first. Perching on a wall to stare out over the water, through the water. Seeing something only it could see. A rustle of branches said another raven had arrived, a tree its perch. Two more eyes to pierce the water also looking for what they alone would see.

With a low croak the first raven took flight. At first flying high then swooping low it skimmed over water almost as dark as itself before giving another croak, calling to the other who answered back as it too took flight. The two of them swooped over the river and then soared high to screech what might have been an invitation or an order. A message to the other ravens heading towards them.

Ten, fifteen, twenty; nobody counted. Nobody could. Just a cloud of black in the distance moving against the wind as, slowly, the shape resolved into individual ravens. Flying low now they circled, they dived, they circled again before taking rest on the bare tree branches. All of them staring at the river as it rippled in the chill wind. Its secrets kept to itself in defiance of the ravens.

Like the crowds the birds now fell silent, waiting as if for a signal. A sign to be received. Until then they would bide their time and wait. When it came, they would be ready. That was their purpose.

There was a hush, felt by all. A hush of wonder, of anticipation. Then the first raven spoke, its croak brash and cruel, commanding obedience.

Answered by all their cries echoed across the river, coming back from the water which otherwise continued to ignore them. Again, they called, each of them in their own time and to no set rhythm. Calls that jangled the nerves of those listening, that reached to the very bone. Calls that were loud and long; harsh, insistent. Calls that spoke to the soul of all those there. Calls that were terrifying. Commanding to all but the river, still defying them.

Still and dark it stayed as, slowly, the ravens fell silent. Their calls still harsh, but infrequent, quieter. More question than order they spoke perhaps to each other, perhaps to God, seeking an answer that soon came. Where it came from no-one would know, but beyond doubt it arrived. The proof of it being the first raven taking flight followed by five others.

Low over the water they flew, circling a patch of water that stayed calm, ignoring them until they spoke once more. Their six-fold cries answered by every raven there they spoke again, and again. Answered every time.

Croaks so harsh, so insistent, not even the river could disobey. There were too many and their commands too powerful to be resisted. It had no choice but to obey and slowly, reluctantly, it did. The water finally giving up what only the ravens could see.

No-one else could, not at first. For them the river stayed just as dark and impenetrable. Then, at last, they saw a movement in the water. A disturbance. A shape, vague at first, rising from

4

the depths, coming to the surface where it could be clearly seen for what it was: a corpse, face down, lifeless.

At sight of it the ravens fell silent; their work done. Now they could leave it to the boat being rowed towards what were just the mortal remains of whoever it had been. The once living man being watched by the ravens that stood silently, respectfully. Black clad pall bearers standing in mute witness as strong arms pulled the body on board.

Once it left the water, once the corpse was safely back in the hands of Man, the ravens took flight. Seemingly without pattern they flew, filling the air with the sound of beating wings. Darkening the sky, they scattered; flying in all directions before wheeling around. Each one of them flying over the cold body before disappearing into the clouds.

Perhaps in search of its departed soul.

CHAPTER ONE

OF MEETINGS AND THEIR CONSEQUENCES

More cellar than place of medicine, the room was long and dark. Bare walls reaching to vaulted ceiling almost without break except for a few semi-circular windows where wall met roof, looking out at ground level onto the pavement outside. In that place they were the only source of daylight available, but on such a cold November day there was very little of that shining through. The sky outside was too dark, which was why gas lights burned fitfully, throwing out as much shadow as light.

In the dimness it was difficult to make out the face of the man slowly walking through that room; his footsteps soft as he walked past vaulted arches all in deep shadow. Only as he came closer to where the lights burned more brightly could it be seen he was a man not yet in his thirtieth year whose black hair curled for reasons of nature not fashion. The look on his face could also be seen as he took the last few steps to the corpse laying on a table in the middle of the room it had been taken to. The dead house, as it was known. The morgue.

With pity, with curiosity and with some reluctance, he

looked at the figure. Then, before it could cast its spell which always kept any mortal man fascinated, he looked at the two men standing beside it who finally acknowledged his presence although not with any friendship. That would be asking too much. One man at least would never regard him with any fondness.

"I thought I might see you today," the man in question told him before turning to the other. "The Press has just arrived."

"Doyle, Ignatius Doyle," the new arrival introduced himself to the other, still a stranger.

"Of *The Chronicle*," the first man spoke again, making it clear they were acquainted.

As indeed they were. The man now looking at Doyle with undisguised irritation was Doctor Stanhope. A physician whose pathologies had lately been regularly interrupted by the reporter he had just addressed. The same reporter who stood his ground calmly before him.

"I ask only for your medical report."

"You do?" The doctor bristled. "Then it's easily settled. He drowned. Now let that be the end of it."

There was a tension between the two men, that was clear. The doctor, easily five and forty with the moustache and the manner which only physicians could comfortably wear, looked hard at the man who asked too many questions for his liking. In return the other said nothing and yet returned the stare without blinking.

As they stood there the silence grew in which, faintly at first, the sound of tapping could be heard. A regular, persistent drumming which came from the window where a raven now stood, its beak tapping against the glass. Its presence as much felt as heard.

Another appeared, then another. Their tapping now louder. Soon others arrived at the next window, and the window after that until what little light there had been was blocked by ravens; all of them knocking against the windows until there could be no hiding from it, no way of ignoring their presence. The sound grew louder, it grew stronger, and then, just as unexpectedly, it stopped. In its place, silence.

The ravens stood mute as they stared into the morgue, witnesses to the proceedings, but to what end only they could know. No human ever could.

"It was how he came to drown," Doyle said softly, breaking the uneasy silence that followed the ravens' tapping.

"As to that the matter is also easily resolved," the other man, as yet to identify himself to Doyle, spoke.

"That's Canon Jefferies," Doctor Stanhope muttered by way of introduction.

In a great coat, tightly buttoned, there was no sign of any clerical garb, yet there was a certain stillness, a calmness, about him which together with the dark silver of his hair spoke of a deeply religious man.

"Your Grace," Doyle addressed him as he waited for further explanation.

In their own way so too did the ravens who stood unmoving in that brief moment of silence before the canon spoke again.

"I have enquired and there were no witnesses to the event."

"Or none who will speak of it," Doyle replied; his voice soft and polite as was only to be expected in the presence of the cloth.

"That may well be the case," Canon Jefferies acknowledged. "Nevertheless, without witnesses to say otherwise we must conclude this was an accident."

His words, like his manner, were calm and yet firm. Equally so was his conviction when he responded to a curious look from Doyle.

"In which case the poor wretch can be given a proper burial. A Christian burial."

Unlike a suicide, in which case he would be denied the sacrament, as Doyle began to realise. With it came understanding. It was pity that motivated him, pity and compassion.

"You make no judgement," he said in a way that was both question and statement.

Perhaps in understanding Canon Jefferies smiled a thin smile.

"I leave any judgement to our Lord," he answered with no trace of doubt. "My ... slight task is to prepare his soul for that event. Everything else I leave to God and his infinite mercy."

His words fell softly into the shadows which swallowed them, deadened them, so that even in such a cavernous cellar there were no echoes. Instead the words and the thoughts they expressed vanished into the darkness beyond the hearing of anyone had they been there to listen. As it was only the ravens overheard, signified by the way their heads slowly bowed before the man of God. An act almost of reverence yet witnessed by no-one.

For sure Doyle gave it no notice. Yet even he bowed his head before the canon in a gesture of respect and understanding before he spoke of more secular matters.

"An accident as you would have it," he began slowly, "for which reason the constabulary would have no cause to investigate further, nor any other judged to be accidental of which there have been a few lately."

Was it his words or the sudden loud croaking of a raven as if in agreement with them that made the canon start? For sure only he and his God would ever know what caused the sudden jerk of his head, or the wide-eyed stare; both of them gone in the merest of seconds and unnoticed by the two men with him. Distracted by raven call they had turned away momentarily in search of its source with the effect that they missed such an unexpected change in the canon. Only when they turned back did they see he now wore a thoughtful, troubled, expression.

"There has been no talk of foul play," he answered slowly.

"And no sign of it either," the doctor growled.

"Nevertheless..." Doyle trailed off, finding no cause to say more. It was the tone of his voice and the look on his face that posed the question. Because of it he was able to speak quietly, respectfully still. Even so his words were again followed by raven call and then another to the visible distress of the canon.

Seeing that the doctor turned back towards the ravens his arms making wild gestures intended to drive them away. Actions that were on the whole ignored. The ravens stayed motionless although, perhaps because of it or for reasons of

10

their own, they fell silent. No longer did they call out, instead they watched with unblinking eyes as the canon composed himself.

At last he spoke again.

"Such considerations are for later. Firstly, I propose to discover if this man has any relatives so the funeral arrangements can be made," he said in the air of one who has reached a decision.

"Then you'd best be quick about it," the doctor advised with a glance at the lifeless body. "There's a pretty penny lying there and it wouldn't do to trust everyone."

He had no need to explain further. Left unattended the corpse was at risk from those once known as Resurrection Men who had once sold the dead to those who would further their medical studies, but who now plied their trade, if trade it could be called, under a different guise. They had even taken corpses from the very graves themselves so they could be sold to hospitals, or even doctors, in furtherance of their anatomical training. Now, after Parliament had passed an Act stating that the remains of those without family, or worse without money, could be claimed for the cause of education.

As a way of protecting those safely in their coffins the Act had indeed worked the way it was intended although as the demand for such cadavers would always be high, as was reflected in the price paid for each one, there were some who would not hesitate if the body went unclaimed for too long. The destitute freely claimed by science was not enough to satisfy the demands of the medical profession.

Knowing this the canon smiled nodded briefly. "Best it be

done straight away," he agreed and then glanced quickly at Doyle. "Come with me from this place. I would talk with you."

It was said quietly, almost a whisper, yet there was no hiding the seriousness of the intent behind it. Canon Jefferies was a troubled man. His voice, his face, even his very demeanour all showed it plainly.

As if to acknowledge this Doyle nodded wordlessly and fell in step beside the man of God to walk with him out of the cellar mortuary. As they did so Doctor Stanhope shook his head in resignation at the sight before turning his attention back to the body lying on the table in front of him. His final thought was that the canon must know what he was doing, but no good would come of it. Some things were best left alone in his opinion.

As for the ravens he gave them no thought nor even the slightest glance. Had he done so he would have seen them standing motionless, staring intently at the canon until he was swallowed by the shadows. Then, once he was lost to the sight of mortal man, they silently disappeared from the windows. There was somewhere else they needed to be; something else they needed to do.

For such reason they left their pavement lookout to fly round the building before coming to rest on the bare branches of the trees at its entrance. Few though they were they still offered a secure perch. A vantage point from which they could watch as Canon Jefferies and Doyle appeared at the door.

Walking together as they were, and talking only of the cold wind blowing about them, they took no notice of the dark observers. Their attention, what little they could spare of it, was on the bare flagstones rather than the trees flanking them. They turned to face each other. A chilly place to stop and talk yet stop and talk they did.

"You wished to speak with me," Doyle spoke softly with the question in his voice if not his words.

Before the canon could speak a raven chose to answer for him. Its croak, soft and melancholy, floated over them, seeming to linger before being dispersed by the chill wind. Doyle turned towards its source at which he finally saw the ravens now on every tree; all of them looking towards the two men. Their attention entirely on them.

As if seeking an answer Doyle turned back to the canon who nodded gently.

"A storytelling."

"Your pardon," Doyle replied completely at a loss.

In explanation the canon nodded towards the birds. "A group of ravens is known as a Storytelling," he paused a brief moment and then added, "Some would say it's an unkindness of ravens, but my preference is a storytelling."

Here Doyle nodded. "And whose story are they telling?"

"Ours most like," the canon answered, suddenly serious. "Or perhaps just mine."

Strange words which made Doyle look at him closely. Perhaps by instinct or perhaps taking his lead from the ravens he said nothing, content to wait for the canon to speak again.

The wait, if it could be called that, lasted but seconds after which the canon gave him a strange look.

"Your words," he began, then paused, searching for the word. "Your words disturbed me," he continued after

13

noticeable delay. "You raised doubts in my mind," he finished as yet another soft raven call drifted over them.

Like before it remained. An almost ghostly presence seemingly trapped by the ravens themselves, making it stay above the two men. The echo of it touching their very souls. This was no mere raven call. It was bewitching, in acknowledgement of which the canon nodded slowly, in understanding.

"As you say many souls have been lost of late," he said, his words chosen carefully as though he was only just now having the thoughts he needed to express. "So many that perhaps some other agency is involved, some other cause masked by my good intentions," he continued and then abruptly became more business-like. "Come. I'll know if there's devilish work afoot here and I'm charging you with the finding out. You'll take my commission?"

As he spoke there was a hush. No wind blew. No raven moved. All was quiet. A stillness descended as if God and all his creatures were waiting for the answer from Doyle.

Yet taken aback as he was at first, he had none to give. With his own thoughts freshly arrived he could do no more than look at the canon.

"The matter needs looking into," he said slowly. "If it be Satan's work you shall know, but know also if the hand of Man is involved my first duty is to the constabulary. The law should know first, as should the readers of my newspaper."

"I can expect no more," the canon nodded, a slight smile on his lips. "I'll know the truth of the matter even if I have to read it in the pages of *The Chronicle*."

His smile continued to show the words were kindly meant.

No offence was intended nor, if much could be inferred by the slight nod Doyle gave him in return, was any taken. Rather the two men sealed their pact with the briefest of handshakes and agreed they would meet again. Then, that done, they both went their separate ways, each deep in their own thoughts.

So deep neither of them noticed the ravens had completely disappeared. Even if they had it would have signified nothing, not then. Later they would understand, but until then they went about their business and ignored the ravens as has always been the way of mortal man. They had other, more worldly, things to concern them.

One such thing being the wind which blew cold that night, cold with flecks of snow. The kind of icy wind that cut through even the warmest of coats and quickened the pace of all those whose lot was to be out of doors. The sooner to be by fireside.

On that night no-one could think of anything else. For sure not Doyle whose brisk steps took him through narrow city streets which formed maze-like in that far from reputable area. This was a place of the poor, of the destitute. A badly lit, badly ventilated series of streets whose usual occupants were, for the most part, as unhealthy as the air they breathed.

Like all good folk Doyle knew this, except in his case it was not known as a place to avoid. It was a place from whence came so many of the stories for his newspaper. That was why he knew it so well although that night with his thoughts elsewhere he chose to ignore all those he passed who in their turn chose to ignore him.

Only half seen in the darkness, and considered even less, they each followed their own path, caring nothing for the lives of others. It was that kind of night. It was that kind of city. It was all kinds of city where such behaviour was commonplace.

In parts prosperous, in parts not, it was no different from any other and given no thought by its citizens. Each with their own purpose they thought of nothing else and expected no more of others. As with all cities it was full of strangers who had no inclination to stop and talk even supposing there was someone who would listen.

In some ways too that described Doyle this particular night. At such a time, and in such weather, his only thought was the ale house he was heading towards. That and the log fire he knew it would have blazing. Finally, but only when he arrived, did he think about the man he was to meet there.

Even in the crowd the man was easily spotted. Tall and broad he carried an air of command which marked him out as a member of the constabulary despite him not being in uniform. It was the swagger, the expectation of not being challenged which set him apart in that way. Most likely it was also why he was able to command a seat at a table comfortably close to the fire.

For sure it was also why, slice of meat pie in his hand, he was able to look across that same table at Doyle without hint of shame or apology.

"This is good," he said, waving the pie slice as a way of showing to what he was referring. "You should try some."

"Since it was bought with my coin," Doyle murmured in reply.

At this the man cocked his head to one side, considering the matter for a moment before grinning, giving a brief nod and then taking another bite of pie. He was a man who liked his food. The more so if someone else was prepared to do the paying and he knew Doyle would always pay. He even knew why.

He was a sergeant in the constabulary. Sergeant Frasier, to give him a name. Tobias as Doyle believed he was called although he had never used that name himself. Theirs was too much a professional relationship for any such informality. One would provide the food and the ale and in return the other would provide information.

"Can't beat a good death," the sergeant grinned again in ghoulish good humour. "There's always someone who wants to know more."

"Concerning this?" Doyle looked at him in surprise.

The sergeant nodded. "Or in her case wanting to tell more. Madame Clara. You've heard of her?"

To show he did indeed know the name Doyle nodded. "*The Chronicle* carries her advertising."

He spoke now with more disappointment than surprise. Madame Clara, renowned mystic in her own advertising at least, could be almost expected to take an interest in such matters. There was no mystery in that.

"She said the spirits were disturbed," the sergeant added in between ale and pie.

"As she would," Doyle muttered; his next question already framed when the sergeant gave him a peculiar look.

"The time before that it was the sister," he said in a musing, reflective air as if he too was curious. "She came back too."

At this Doyle paused, needing a moment for thought.

"The sister of this latest, do I have to call it an accident?"

The sergeant shook his head. "The one before that."

Intrigued, Doyle leant forward. It seemed someone else was taking an interest in this sudden spate of what, with all due respect to God and clergymen, he still thought of as suicides.

"And she came back you say?"

Seeing his interest, the policeman smiled. Honest soul that he was he liked to know he was earning his meal.

"Wanted to know if there was any connection, but no investigation had been started so we had nothing to tell her. Only that Madame Clara was interested too so she went off to see her."

There Sergeant Frasier stopped long enough to laugh.

"Looks like you'll have to do the same if you want to meet her, and you should definitely meet her. She's a comely lady by all accounts."

He finished with what could have been a leer had it not been obscured by the glass now at his lips. The look in his eyes mischievous. For his part Doyle took no offence at this as it was in the manner of the man and would, in any case, have been pointless. He was incorrigible.

It should also be said Doyle had more pressing matters on his mind at that moment of which the greatest was the thought that, regardless of his inclination, he would have to seek out the mystic.

"It would appear I have little choice in that matter," he muttered as much to himself as to his companion of the table.

So saying he stood up to leave the man to his pie and ale. There was nothing more to be gained from this conversation so he had no more reason to stay. Even so as he saw the curious, almost suspicious, look on the face of the policeman he felt compelled to add, "There's something amiss here and I've been commissioned to find out what it is."

Satisfied at that Sergeant Frasier smiled with little humour. "You'd best hope it's not the spirits or they might get to you first. Then where'll you be."

Where indeed. Certainly not where he knew he must go next and just as certainly not to meet the person whom he knew he had to meet. Madame Clara that is, whose door he was now standing outside waiting to be admitted.

As has already been said the house of Madame Clara was not a place Doyle ever expected to be and yet he was there. Not by choice, it has to be admitted, nor was he comfortable with the notion. Even so he was there. How else could he make the acquaintance of the woman who, if Sergeant Frasier was to be believed, was also taking an interest in these fatalities? How else would he be able to hear her story.

Indeed, that was the quandary facing him. Only by going through Madame Clara could he hope to meet this other woman and yet Madame Clara had no reason to be co-operative. Quite the contrary. In truth she had much to gain by keeping them separate or at the least in controlling the circumstances of their meeting. A plain fact known to them both.

"Why would *The Chronicle* be interested in such a respectable lady?" she asked and much as Doyle would have liked to refuse her he knew better.

"Her brother died recently," he answered hoping the

candid nature of his smile would disguise the fact he had told her nothing except that which she already knew.

In that he was frustrated as she looked back at him with a sly smile on her lips.

"Tragically too."

"Which is why *The Chronicle* might wish to discuss the matter with her."

Doyle made sure not to express any emotion in his voice, certainly no eagerness. That would be to give Madame Clara too much power which is why he calmly sipped his tea and smiled at the maid who served it. Anything to allay her suspicions that more might be involved.

Small and plump she may have been, but nevertheless it was a shrewd and calculating woman he was dealing with. Her dress was not the flowing and much decorated robes of others in her line of business, but as sober and demure as any other respectable member of her gender. So much so that to those not of her acquaintance she had the appearance of, perhaps, a widow in straightened circumstances; certainly nothing less than a seamstress. In short there was nothing to betray her profession, although as innocent as she might appear, it would not do to underestimate her which was why he strove to maintain an air of only the slightest curiosity. A passing interest, no more.

In that, however, his actions were in vain. Despite his efforts her own curiosity rose.

"You think she may have a story to tell?"

Madame Clara was still looking for information which Doyle had already determined not to give.

For which reason he merely shrugged. "That has yet to be discovered."

"And yet you would meet with her."

His answer already prepared, Doyle smiled. "How else could I know? It is true her tale may be of only slight value, but it has always been in the nature of my profession to be a snapper-up of ill-considered trifles."

His words brought a smile from the woman who sat facing him. Here was no innocent to be easily misled, she realised. This was someone who would be much harder for her to handle. For this reason, after no more than a moment or two of thought, she changed her strategy.

"But what if a respectable lady has no wish to be the subject of stories in a newspaper?" she asked, her face all innocence.

"Then I would respect her wishes," Doyle replied before softly adding, "Assuming I could be certain they were indeed her wishes."

"For which the lady would have to be contacted," Madame Clara continued to smile as she saw how the game could be played to her own advantage. "By me if you will."

"Her address is all I ask," Doyle murmured for all the world expecting no less although in his heart he knew better.

The way Madame Clara shook her head was proof enough of that.

"No," she answered, her words the merest murmur. "That would never do. The lady would never thank me for giving her address to a stranger, not even one so handsome."

She finished with the smile of a coquette at which Doyle could only bow his head before saying, "Then I see no way forward."

They watched each other, each with their own thoughts.

"Perhaps there could be." She smiled her softest smile. "I shall intercede on your behalf."

At her words Doyle sensed a trap, yet he could do no more than smile innocently.

"How so?"

Her smile, cat-like, in return was all satisfaction. "I shall speak to the lady on your behalf. We are to meet anyway as I have already agreed to use such gifts as I possess to contact her brother's spirit. If she consents you too shall be present at the time. In that way you will be able to meet the lady."

"You are too kind," Doyle replied, wondering how he might extricate himself from what he perceived to be a delicate situation. A meeting perhaps in a tearoom or similar establishment would have been more to his liking as he was about to say, but Madame Clara would have none of it.

"Then it's settled," she announced before adding with a sly smile, "And I'm sure the readers of *The Chronicle* would be most interested in your account."

There he had it. Now he knew the price of her co-operation yet he could see no way out of it. Helpless in the face of it as he was it seemed his only option was to accept her terms.

"*The Chronicle* will always publish anything it believes to be worthy," he told her, hoping that in some small way this would allow for sufficient excuse should the account not be published for reasons of it not being written.

At that, however, she frowned slightly.

"But your account, from one who was there, would surely be of much interest," she looked at him, pressing for his agreement.

"I can only report on such events as they happen," he murmured in his own defence. "I cannot write them in advance, or decide on their worthiness."

"I wouldn't presume any other. Still, I'm sure I can trust to your good judgement and, dare I say, to your honour."

After which the bargain, if it could be called that, was sealed. Helpless as he was in her scheming Doyle could only agree her terms in the certain knowledge of what was to come. At a time of her choosing, which he knew would be soon, he would be invited to witness her attempt to contact the spirits. What would transpire on that particular occasion he had no idea other than the thought that, in return, she expected an account of it to appear in *The Chronicle* for her further advancement. Yet, unhappy as he was at the thought of it, there was no other way for him to meet the woman he was looking for. Madame Clara had made sure of that. She would be in charge of the encounter and she would profit as a result.

Even so the situation was not without a certain dark comedy. How else to describe it. After all, despite himself he would be communing with the spirits to further the commission of a clergyman. Could the affair he had so willingly embarked on be any stranger?

A question only the ravens could answer.

CHAPTER TWO

A DARK NIGHT AND A DARKER EVENT

There may have been a full moon that night, but few would remember it. Only those whose business was the compiling of almanacs, or those who read them, would ever know for sure. No-one else would know, not unless by chance their eyes were on the heavens when some stray gust of wind parted the clouds long enough for it to become visible.

For the most part the moon and its light was hidden which is to say the night was dark; the clouds thick and coal-black through which no celestial illumination could penetrate. With the sun itself long since dropped beneath the horizon, all heavenly light, all that provided by God, was hidden behind thick veils. The result being that which would hide from such things was free to roam. The lights of man had no such check on its activities.

A simple fact and yet one given no consideration by the mortal men. So sure were they of their own superiority they believed in only that which they could see and thought themselves safe beneath the flickering gas lights of their own cities. Had they known the truth of it, of course, they would have known that the light kept them safe only from other men; assailants, footpads, murderers. From all other dark forces they would be forever vulnerable.

Worse still, not knowing their vulnerability, they thought themselves to be safe and so took themselves to places only the foolhardy would go. In another way of saying had they known they would have stayed away, or been foolhardy. It was their not knowing which made them do it; thinking nothing of the danger involved because they failed to recognise it. How else to explain what happened next?

In the way of all such affairs it began in a quiet manner. There was no warning or hint of what was to follow such as that found in the popular theatre. No orchestra prepared the way for what was to come nor did any villainous dialogue set the scene. It was simply a night, dark and cold, where a man could be seen walking in the false belief the streetlamps kept him safe.

What Doyle, for it was he, was doing could also be easily explained. In that at least there was no mystery as he was simply doing what all members of his profession could be expected to do. He was visiting the scene where such events as he intended to report on had taken place. Plainly put he intended to examine the bridge from which more than one soul had chosen to depart from this world.

A more knowing man would have waited for daylight, but no mortal man could have been expected to know that. To be precise no mortal man could know why. Such knowledge belonged elsewhere. Even the awareness that such arcane knowledge existed had long since been lost. For sure Doyle had no inkling of it as he impulsively took the decision after leaving the house of Madame Clara.

So it was that his footsteps led him to the fateful site. Not directly, it should be said. There was some distance between the two, but eventually and after much locomotion he found himself approaching the bridge in question.

In age, no more than a score of years, it had been built entirely for reasons of commerce. Because of it all manner of items produced in all manner of factories and mills could be more easily transported to any such place as would take them. At an agreed price somewhat naturally. For which reasons the city grew more prosperous and the good burghers considered the bridge to be a sound investment.

On its upper deck, if it could be so described, were the iron rails for the steam trains which regularly carried passengers and goods from station to destination. This, as might be guessed, was the prime function for the bridge. If not its only purpose definitely its main purpose. Evidence of which Doyle was able to witness for himself while still some distance away.

Stopping for a while at the relentless growl of approaching train he heard and then saw it. The night train on its way to the capital and various other cities in between. Thundering across the bridge, the smoke from its smokestack lit by brief flakes of fire, it was the very symbol of engineering might. Powerful, unassailable, there was no greater force, in the world of Man at least.

Outside of such narrow confines, however, other forces were far greater, but only the ravens would ever see them. Only they would see forces, dark and malevolent, beyond their power to control. Beyond even their power to resist. All they could do was warn; their task since creation began.

A daunting task to be sure, yet necessary as through the eyes of Doyle there was nothing to be seen. Just a bridge, dimly lit. Beneath it the river, unmoving apart from the occasional ripple where cold wind disturbed dark water. To the one side of it, on his right as he approached it, that same river stretched through the city lapping against warehouses and factory alike.

To his left the river grew even wider. Somewhere, beyond the place where dark water merged with dark sky, there was a bend. A curve to the far side of which was the port. There life was all a hustle and bustle as ships of all sizes loaded and unloaded all manner of cargoes. Wealth, and the fruits of that wealth, being delivered to the satisfaction and profit of all.

There too the lights were bright and people busy. Not so the stretch of water over which the bridge spanned. There the lights were few, the people fewer still and tall buildings blocked all evidence of any such commerce. As has already been said it was dark. A darkness only the eyes of ravens could pierce.

They alone could see the dark shape slowly taking form over the water. A greater blackness against the dark. Like a mist it slowly appeared, spreading out over the river. Beginning from the bend which hid the port it grew, growing relentlessly; reaching ever further towards the bridge.

Thinly spread to begin with, it expanded. It thickened. More appeared. Thick tendrils stretching out, reaching upwards; reaching for the bridge and all those on it. Fresh victims being hunted.

Silent, unnoticed, the vile mass spread itself across the river.

From bank to bank it lay there, pulsating, before gathering itself up. A plume of evil rising steadily higher. Towering up, pulling in the darkness as it steadily rose. Reaching the underside of the bridge it flowed along the length of it. Around it. Over it. Through it

All the while human eyes saw nothing. Oblivious to the danger, they went about their business thinking only of themselves, or those they were about to meet. Not even Doyle, there to study the surroundings, detected anything untoward. He saw, in fact, only the bridge he had seen countless times before and had given it no consideration.

To him it was still just a structure of stone and metal. On its upper deck, as has already been described, were the railway lines. Beneath it a road for pedestrians and such transport as was drawn by horses not steam. It was, therefore, a tunnel of sorts lit by the occasional lamp at night and by the sun during the day. Along its length there were many places where its sides were open to the air. A metal railing the only barrier between the bridge and the water so far below.

This, it should be said, is what Doyle intended to study. The place apparently chosen by those unfortunate souls who had determined to end their lives and were just as determined to see it through. A dark quest indeed and yet one which was bound by compassion for in this way he hoped to gain at least some measure of insight into their fatal decision. The better to explain it and, possibly, even prevent further occurrences.

So intent was he on this he failed to see the raven flying towards him as he crossed the almost deserted road leading to the bridge. Only when it called out, its croak loud and strident, did he look up to see it. Mainly in surprise it has to be said yet he looked, curious for a second or perhaps two, and then he ignored it.

With no reason to consider what could have been a warning, or an order, he walked on ignoring even the impatient croak of the ignored bird. Beneath him a dark shadow rose inexorably to the bridge; seen by the ravens, but not by the man. Unknowingly he walked on, the blackness now spreading across the underside of the bridge.

Three ravens now perched on its stonework. Their calls loud, insistent, and also ignored. Dark tendrils now creeping onto the roadway, more ravens screeched yet more warnings. All of them misunderstood by the man about to start crossing the bridge.

Walking slowly, his thoughts elsewhere, no raven call reached Doyle. Nothing could, except, as he stood on the threshold, he stopped to look in wonder at the strange behaviour of another already on the bridge. Another man only just reached manhood by his looks. Certainly he was no more than a few years beyond. What his original purpose had been in crossing the bridge was unknown, and always would be, for he was no longer attempting any such thing. Instead he was standing, staring into the darkness as his whole body shook uncontrollably.

Unwillingly it seemed he took a step towards the edge only to draw back again, his arms waving about him. For all the world it appeared as if he was being dragged by hands unseen. Hands seen by ravens, but not by Doyle who, to his horror, saw the young man climbing the railing. He was about to throw himself into the river below.

Not yet affected by the miasma, Doyle ran forward. A raven call in his ears. A call to action or a warning he had no idea which, nor did he give it any thought; his only concern being to reach the man in time.

Mercifully the distance was short. A few paces only and Doyle had his arms around the man, dragging him to safety. Away from the edge and the sheer fall to the water below.

As he did so he looked into a face contorted with abject fear. He gripped Doyle tightly, breath rasping in his throat. As if in the final throes of exhaustion he stayed there sobbing with relief, or release of overpowering emotions more like. This was no poor wretch intent on his own destruction. This was a soul in bondage.

Now, released from whatever dark bonds held him, he stepped back to look at Doyle. His mouth moved as if in speech yet no words came forth. Still incapable of such things he could only stare wildly about at the bridge, at the night, at the ravens. His head shaking as he tried in vain to make any sense of it all.

Suddenly he stopped, eyes ablaze. For no more than a second he stood rigid until, without conscious decision, he turned and ran. Thoughtlessly, in panic, he raced across the bridge, desperate to be away from whatever darkness had possessed him. Not even when he reached the end of the bridge did he stop. Still he ran on into the night, soon to be lost forever as the city itself swallowed him up, losing him in its side streets where he would be safe. Or rather, where the only danger would come from men. In that respect, of course, he would still be at risk, but his peril would at least be of a mortal danger. No longer would he be under any influence from that dark entity he had so recently been subject to and for him, on that night, it would suffice.

Doyle stood for a moment, capable only of staring after him. These were peculiar events indeed yet try as he might he could find neither explanation nor understanding. The entire episode had him completely at a loss.

All of it so far beyond his reasoning, he gave it no more thought, as strange as that was for a man of his profession. Its very nature being that of which newspaper accounts are made he should have been expected to look into it further. He should have questioned and there is no doubt in a different place he would, except, without him realising it, a strange lethargy came over him. No longer could he take an interest.

Seen through the eyes of ravens a dark cloud was about him. A formless evil far beyond their power had him in its grip from which there would be no escape they could engineer. No living creature could. Certainly not Doyle himself.

He was trapped. Lost to the mortal world. Around him the darkness thickened and as it did his despair grew. A depression almost of insanity taking over his very soul, making him see life in all its futility. Clearly now he could see his own life, the lives of others and how little they all counted.

Nothing mattered to him anymore; nothing signified at all as he looked out into the darkness, the river suddenly inviting. What had he to live for? What had anyone? This was his only thought as he took a first, unwilling step forward.

His soul steeped in darkness, he was unable to resist, unable to keep away from the railing and the river beneath it, his steps taking him ever closer. Except, even as he did something deep within him stirred. A fugitive hope that stopped him, made him pull back. This was not the answer, it seemed to say, but all the while a greater force said it was.

Gripped ever tighter he was being pulled, dragged, towards the edge. His footsteps taking him ever closer to the iron railing, to the river which would grant him release from all his worldly cares. Still some small part of him fought against it, but to no avail. As he grasped the railing in one last final effort to resist he knew there could only be one outcome. He was doomed.

Beyond help of man, or of raven, he stood, his body rigid. Chest heaving as his breath came hard. His last few breaths before he gave himself to the river; before it claimed him. His last few seconds of mortal life.

As it would have been if not for other forces which were at work that night. Forces as merciful as the dark cloud was malign. Not summoned by ravens nor by prayer yet it appeared when it was all over for Doyle. At the last he was rescued.

There was no sign, no sense of it, just a sudden gust of wind which parted the clouds. Not everywhere, and not for long, but it was enough. The night sky cleared allowing the moon to shine through, its beams lighting up the city, the bridge, turning the entire river to silver.

This was no light of Man. This was light from God. A light of celestial power, more than the dark cloud could withstand. More than it could fight.

Under its beams the dark cloud shrank, shrivelled. Falling away from Doyle. His senses returning, he looked around no longer thinking of the river. That was gone. In its place: the call of a raven.

Only they knew the respite was but short-lived. Soon the clouds would return and with them would come the darkness. The darkness in which the greater blackness could flourish. Before then, as the ravens alone knew, Doyle had to reach safety. If not, no power could save him twice.

For such reason a second raven flew over him. Its call neither loud nor harsh, but capable of reaching him still. At the sound of it he looked up, befuddled yet in understanding and set off in their direction. Reeling like a drunkard he staggered, almost fell, as step by far too slow step the bridge was crossed.

Above him wisps of cloud were covering the moon. Below him the darkness was starting to grow. Around him the ravens, not daring to get too close. In the midst of it all: him. A frail mortal man only vaguely aware he was in a race where his very soul was the prize.

Every step taking him closer to safety, his head now clearing, he ran on. In his mind nothing other than the ravens who seemed to be calling him, spurring him to fresh efforts. Their calls urgent. A dozen paces, less, until he reached the end of the bridge.

Then the world went dark. The moon now obscured. With the light from God extinguished no longer was there a check on the black cloud. Nothing to hold it at bay, it grew. It grew in size. It grew in strength. It grew in hunger. Its dark tendrils again reaching out, not for the bridge. This time their target was Doyle.

Already he could feel it, calling for him, pulling him back.

Dark voices attacking his very being. The fear in him rising because of it, yet that same fear drove him on. No longer needing any urging from the ravens, he ran.

Across the bridge, still he ran. The main road he was on looking cold and unfriendly to his eyes. There was no safety there. He knew it and at that thought he was lost. Lost, that is, until a raven circled ahead of him before darting into a side alley. There it turned, re-appeared, called and then flew back into the alleyway.

The meaning obvious, Doyle followed it without thought. Down a flight of stone steps he ran, then another. Occasionally colliding with the side wall, no longer knowing where he was going or why, fear alone drove him, pushing him on until he emerged into a cobbled square. There he stopped to catch his breath, only to hear the ravens' call again.

They knew, as he never would, that the dark cloud had left the bridge. Settling thick over the water it oozed. It came up and over the bank; a long mass of darkness which already had the taste of Doyle and wanted more.

Far from safe, with the cloud rising above him, he saw a raven flying across the square to another side alley. A place even he knew he had to be. A small side street that seemed to offer nothing but the entrance to another square. For the most part buildings, houses. There seemed to be nothing else there, except in the far corner he saw a graveyard.

The ravens were heading there so Doyle followed. The dark cloud behind him as he saw and understood. Beyond the graveyard stood a chapel. Sanctuary.

Another raven, another call, showed him the open door.

His way into a place that was holy, consecrated, safe. A place where not even the darkness could penetrate. In there he would be safe, but only if he could reach it before the blackness took him.

It was there, hard on his heels; the ravens scattering ahead of it. Across the graves it flowed, relentless in its pursuit of the man only just out of reach. Every second bringing it closer to him while that same second brought him closer to safety.

A safety reached. With little to spare he dashed across the threshold that would hold the darkness back. There, beyond its grasp, he could stop and catch his breath, for the moment able to do no more. One hand against the wall for its support and his head low, he stood drawing in large breaths with all thought beyond him.

Did the building really shake as the darkness vented its fury against it or was that just in the imagination of a man slipping to the floor where he lay in a swoon? Like so much else about that night Doyle would never know. His senses gone he lay there unmoving, but safe.

Later, much later, when his wits returned, he sat up and looked about him. Gone were the dark clouds and gone too was any sense of evil. The night was now clear and moonlit. In all there was a sense of calm, of peace, which Doyle could feel around him as it soothed his shattered nerves and quietened his beating heart.

About to stand up, he heard a scratching sound coming from the still open door. Turning towards it he saw a single raven standing there, its eyes on him. At that moment he understood. He understood their purpose and he knew their intent. Furthermore, as he returned its stare the raven also knew that he understood.

At which its head bobbed in undeniable satisfaction.

CHAPTER THREE

STORIES AND PLANS

It was in the church where Doyle found him, Canon Jefferies. At the time presumably discussing clerical matters with another clergyman. Whom the other was Doyle had no idea, nor was he introduced. At sight of him Canon Jefferies quickly excused himself from the conversation, but not before giving Doyle a quick look which plainly said this was not a matter for other ears to hear. The canon obviously wanted their arrangement to be kept secret.

This being more or less Doyle's view as well, he raised no objection and walked with the canon to his rooms while discussing issues of such import as the cold weather and the chances of snow. That which might be described as the most usual, or common, subject of conversation. It has, after all, been observed that the one thing which links even the highest born to the lowest in this country is their mutual fascination with the weather. In this it seems we are all alike with Doyle and the canon being no exception.

Only when they were safely in his rooms and privacy was assured did the canon turn to the other matters for which they were both there.

"Must I buy a copy of *The Chronicle*?" he asked with a slight smile which, nevertheless, failed to hide his anxiety.

"I cannot see this as being suitable for the pages of a newspaper," Doyle replied.

By the troubled look on his face as he spoke those few words the canon saw there was much more to this story. More, indeed, than Doyle seemed prepared to tell.

"So not the hand of Man," he murmured, with a feeling of dread at the thought of whatever tale Doyle might have to tell.

Doyle could only shake his head, unsure how to begin.

"Then what?" Canon Jefferies asked softly, uneasily.

Before replying Doyle took a breath. Unbidden his thoughts flew back to that night and the way he had sat in his lodgings afterwards shaking like a man with the ague, a malady beyond even the restorative powers of brandy. Certainly, events such as those beyond even his wildest reckoning were not easy to contemplate, far less discuss. Properly speaking they should have been consigned to that part of the human psyche where all bad memories are stored, never to be talked of again. There they would have stayed, appearing only in the darkest nightmare, except that was not to be his fate as Doyle well knew. The canon wanted an answer.

Doyle found himself struggling for words so that all he could say was, "Something ... evil. Devilish."

Simple as those words were, they clearly struck the canon like a blow. Ashen faced he sat back to stare at the other who could only look back at him just as disturbed.

"Tell me all," Canon Jefferies said at length, trepidation

evident in his voice. "I must know."

Doyle now did so as best he could. Even if, as he knew, it sounded more like the ravings of a madman still he told Canon Jefferies of all that had happened. The man deserved to know although at its conclusion Doyle began to wonder if, perhaps, the story should have remained a secret. Might it not have been an act of kindness to keep the truth hidden.

On that basis there may have been some justification although, in truth, the canon was unlikely to have thanked him. No matter how painful the story he insisted on knowing it in full. Indeed, there were times when he stopped to question Doyle on even the smallest of details, all the while making it clear he should be spared nothing. Nevertheless, Doyle had misgivings.

Judging by his completely pallid face the canon was taking this hard. By all appearances it was as if his very faith was being tested. On one occasion his hand even stole towards a crucifix as if needing its blessing before being snatched back by a man who seemed to fear the wrath of God. All this being done unconsciously what better way could there be of showing his inner mood and his doubts. The man was in a torment which struck to the very foundation of his being.

Out of pity, therefore, if for no other reason, Doyle sat quietly at the end of his tale until the canon had regained some measure of composure. Not completely by any means, but at least he was able to look at the crucifix without hastily averting his eyes which was an encouragement. The more so when he was finally able to look back at Doyle with a wan smile.

"So, what should we do?" he asked softly.

On this matter Doyle had already given some thought as can be imagined. In truth he had thought of nothing else.

"Knowing as we now do that dark forces are involved, if we were to turn our backs on this then surely we would be damned," he began, then, feeling his answer to be too spiritual he added, "In all conscience how can we allow it to continue?"

"Well said," the canon answered. "Well said indeed. It appears we must fight the devil, but where to start. With the bridge?"

"I think not. In my opinion it came from the river; somewhere towards the docks."

At this the canon nodded. "Perhaps a more suitable place to begin," he said and then gave Doyle a look from which all doubt was removed. "There must have been something which allowed the devil through into this world," he continued, hurriedly now. "We must find out what it was if we are to defeat this evil."

An opinion Doyle could hardly refute. Not only did it come from a man who could be expected to have some knowledge of these matters, in addition he had no better suggestion of his own to put forward. Reason enough for him to simply nod his head in agreement.

"There are people I can talk to," he told the canon. "Perhaps one of them knows of something."

He could have added that in his profession knowing those who could be asked was an essential, if not vital, accomplishment. How else to gather the information which was to him meat and drink. The main component of all newspaper stories furthermore.

To him, therefore, this was no more than an everyday occurrence even if the canon took the matter far more gravely.

"Have a care when you do," he warned Doyle. "These are deep waters we are moving into."

Kindly meant as it was, the warning was still unnecessary. Still with black memories of his previous experience Doyle intended to take every precaution in any of his future dealings.

Nevertheless, he smiled his appreciation of the consideration being shown before saying, "I merely intend to see if the hand of Man is also involved."

"For the pages of your newspaper," the canon smiled back, in measure relieved, yet anxious even so. "It would be well to keep your wits about you," he added. "I am mindful that acting on my behalf has already placed you in mortal danger. I would there was no more of it."

A sentiment with which Doyle was happy to agree. He too had no desire to face such a malignancy again. Even if, as he was beginning to believe, he could count on the help of the ravens he would rather it not be tested. An opinion no doubt the ravens shared even if it could never be told. Much as they had been his saviour their storytelling was for all who would listen. It was not just for him.

They were, after all, only there to warn against the folly of Man in general. Individuals could not necessarily count on such warnings, and protection even less. A fact which, while unknown to Doyle as a surety, he nevertheless surmised and so resolved to have more than a little care about him despite it being daylight and his next destination was to be the docks, a place where there could be more danger from men than from spirits. Of that all could agree. It was in the very nature of the place, or the people who inhabited it.

In that respect the docks of any prosperous city will always be the same. Ships laden with all manner of goods bought by the citizens of that city would arrive and ships laden with all manner of goods they had sold would depart. In between there was the bustle of those ships being loaded or unloaded, of any necessary repairs being carried out and of provisions for the voyage being delivered. There was even the same air of organisation as deck hands for those ships were taken on to replace those who, for reasons unknown and unasked, were not making the return voyage.

It was therefore, as perhaps needs no saying, a place of trade, of business and of commerce. A place where vast numbers toiled each to their own trade or craft. The docks provided employment and livelihood for all, including those whose trade or craft lay far outside the boundaries of the law.

Also as perhaps needs no saying it was a place for theft of all kinds, for smuggling and for more than a few murders. In short like the port of any city it could be as dangerous as it was profitable. The two it seemed inevitably linked in any human endeavour. A fact to which those whose task was to police those docks would readily confirm. Of all the police houses in that city theirs would always be the busiest. The manner of which was a question Doyle now found himself asking.

True to his word he was now seeking out any such strange events as happened prior to the recent spate of what he no longer considered to be suicides. Exactly what they should be called was, for the moment, a question he dared not ask, but he did at least accept those poor souls had not taken their own lives. As he now had cause to know other, darker, agencies were involved. His role was now to find the mechanism by which it all began.

For which reason he was visiting the police house of those docks to question the sergeant there. Sergeant Walters. A dark-haired man past his fortieth year who, in the manner of all those who had given their lives to the constabulary, wore a permanent air of weariness occasioned by having witnessed all the vagaries and vicissitudes of human nature.

Even so he professed to be surprised by Doyle who, it should be said, had just asked a question not often heard in police stations or anywhere else for that matter.

"Something strange which happened just latterly," he repeated with that particular look which only a member of the constabulary can give.

In fairness to the sergeant the docks where he was charged with keeping the peace was a veritable hotchpotch of nationalities, each with their conflicting rivalries, jealousies and enmities in addition to those of the citizenry who worked there on either side of the law. To this must be added the fact that, as ships came and went, the population differed with every change of the tide. Also there were itinerant labourers whose presence could only be described as erratic, just like their employment. All of which formed a heady brew so a great many tales could be told which would fall into that category.

"Perhaps those which lack a satisfactory explanation," Doyle murmured; it being the only other qualification he could offer. In passing he had thought of mentioning ravens, but decided against it. Even though Sergeant Frasier had spoken for him, as he knew, that might have been too much for the honest, God-fearing, soul in front of him.

As it was there seemed to be no need. Sergeant Walters pondered the question for a moment. Then his face cleared.

"There was something," he began, speaking slowly as memories were being recalled. "It might suit."

At which he began his story. A story not set amongst the ships themselves, but nearby, amongst the warehouses. Those vast chambers where goods were stored either awaiting despatch by ship or for onward transmission having been received from other ships. A place of transit as they might be described or, as Sergeant Walters described it, a place rife with lawlessness.

Many times thieves, always in gangs, would attempt to steal the rich merchandise stored there. Often too they would succeed much to the annoyance of the merchants and the chagrin of the police. Also, and at other times, it was the goods themselves which were unlawful by not carrying the required excise stamp to show all due duties had been paid. The fruits of smuggling in other words.

These it was which formed the focus of the story the sergeant was about to tell. A suitably strange story for which even a man as experienced as he had no explanation. Fact enough to make it of interest to Doyle.

It happened one mist-shrouded night when he and his men were to conduct an operation against a notorious gang of smugglers who, it was believed, would be landing their contraband that same night. How they knew that the sergeant was not at liberty to disclose although he did go as far as to say such intelligence was considered to be accurate. For which reason they were to be joined by excisemen whose purpose was to impound any such contraband as might be captured. An ill-fated pairing according to the sergeant who clearly had scant regard for those others. Undisciplined and not above helping themselves to a bottle or two, as he described them.

Nevertheless, orders had been given which he had no choice but to obey. It was not for the sergeant to question the judgement of his superiors. So, on the night in question, and his misgivings aside, the two groups assembled with their purpose at least in common.

As described it was a night more suited for smuggling than for law-keeping. The fog rolled in thick, obscuring what light came from the moon and stars, obscuring even the lights of Man. Beyond more than a few feet both police and excisemen could be discerned only by the lanterns they carried. Not even that after a few feet more. Difficult circumstances indeed for those who would uphold the law. Yet, despite the weather, they were duty bound to do so.

As they knew or had been told somewhere at sea a ship was riding at anchor apparently waiting for the tide to turn. When that happened it would enter the port and open its holds up for inspection as was the law. After which, with all duties paid, the cargo it carried could be unloaded. The cargo it still then carried that is.

Before then, as was known, a smaller boat would be moored alongside the ship while still at sea. Its purpose, simply stated, to take as much of the cargo as it could carry. This then to be carried ashore under cover of darkness without reference to the revenue and most certainly without payment of duty. The savings thus made rendering the entire enterprise worthwhile; highly profitable even.

This was also illegal, as needs no saying, which was why the forces of the law were now arrayed against it. Their intention was to wait for the boat to slip into shore and then, once it moored, to arrest the occupants and seize the contraband. A simple plan to be sure and yet out of it would come the story the sergeant was now about to tell.

Its basis came from not knowing where along the dockside the boat would moor. Other than it would not be in the main port, where the great ships docked, they could have no idea. Not for sure at least. An easy guess was it would be somewhere beyond the main port next to where the warehouses were built, because only at the warehouses were there any facilities for unloading smaller boats. These, it should be said, were for more legitimate cargo being carried up and down the river, but, that notwithstanding, the facilities were there.

All the warehouses had them and, unfortunately for the police, there were a great many to choose from. In which case, put to the guess as they were, they could only spread out; between them trying to guard every place of entry. As a consequence of this they were spread thin, but it was the best they could do, circumstances and weather conspiring against them to restrict their options.

Along the quay in a certain portion of the docks stood a row of warehouses. Each one different from the others and separated by a narrow strip of ground on which high walls had been built. Their original purpose was to mark the boundary between one building and another although on this night they would serve a secondary function by providing hiding places. Somewhere for the police and excisemen to stay out of sight as, with lanterns shielded, they waited in the fog and the dark for the boat to arrive.

Unknown to them it was already on its way. Heading into their trap. Soon it would be with them, but before that, as they waited silently and hidden, they heard voices.

Somewhere in the fog others were calling to each other. Carrying in the night air, their voices furtive, guarded. Up to no good. Apparently more than one gang was engaged in some nefarious activity that night.

Still, though, both police and excisemen held their ground. Now was no time for any distraction no matter how tempting it might be, and tempting it surely was. Activity such as that underneath their noses, so to speak, was almost too much to bear, for the police at any rate. What the excisemen thought of it was not recorded.

Even so, hidden as they were, they could hear everything. The muffled orders being given by some gang leader.

"Steady now."

"Careful with that."

His voice was seemingly everywhere in the fog, like the sounds that accompanied his words. There was the scraping of something being dragged. The rattle of chains. Here and there a muffled oath, but why and against what they could have no idea.

The creaking of wood and the lapping of water told those

hiding that a boat was involved, but as to whether it was being loaded, unloaded or both they could have no clue. No indication at all save for one occasion when after the rattle of chains came the sound of a blow being struck. Then another. Both were followed by a cry, more a whimper of pain whose origin stayed unknown.

What beast was being dealt with so harshly would, it seemed, be forever a mystery. Much as the police burned at the sound of such cruelty their duty was clear. More than that it was upon them. After much time spent waiting the boat, and its contraband, had finally arrived.

Gliding through the mist it came. Almost spectral with mist curling around and over it slowly it took form, appearing out of the fog more like a ghost on the water. Its crew, at first wraith-like, now clearly seen.

For the police and the excisemen there was no mistaking it. This was the boat they were there to apprehend. The prize was within their grasp.

Tensely they watched as the boat drifted silently towards the quay. Its handler too skilled to make the slightest noise even in the dark. Still unmoving they watched as figures jumped ashore, their equally skilled hands quickly securing it. Soon the trap would be sprung, but before then they would wait for the first of the contraband to be carried ashore. Proof the gang did indeed intend to cheat the revenue.

A sound plan and a legal requirement required by the courts. All of which came to nought when the men on the boat stopped their activity to stand as if frozen. They too had heard the other voices which they could have no idea came from some equally criminal enterprise. To their suspicious minds they could only believe it was the excisemen coming for them.

Swiftly now desperate hands reached for the ropes, aiming to set the boat free. Their own freedom depending on it, or so they thought. Unfounded as their suspicions were, at least as far as the other gang was concerned, still it was enough. They intended to flee.

Left with no choice now, the police and excisemen sprang into action, leaving their hiding place with loud shouts. Lanterns unshielded, they ran forward. Others, with more lanterns, following behind. All of them running towards the boat, boarding it to tackle the smugglers.

Not to be taken easily, they fought back. At first overpowering the few who came on board. The fight brief but vicious with victory to the smugglers. Their chance to escape.

The boat lost they jumped ashore, hoping to run, hoping to hide. Not expecting to meet those who would stop them if they could. Those who were now running towards them with more shouts, their cries echoing around the docks.

By now all was confusion. A mist-shrouded mêlée where figures appeared from the fog, where lights appeared in the fog and no-one knew who was who until then. From everywhere came the sound of men running, shouting; men being captured, fighting to escape and shouting warnings to those still at large. These followed by shouts from police and excisemen, calling for assistance, calling instructions, directions of those taking flight. All of it muffled and distorted by fog and buildings.

It was chaos. Certainly, no-one was able to take command. For the most part the activities of the night lay hidden to all, police and criminals alike. That was, at least, until the shouts gradually died away to signify the gang members had either been apprehended or escaped. Then silence of a kind fell. There were still sounds of men breathing heavily after their exertions and the occasional curse, but, that aside, the night was silent and calm was restored. The forces of law and order were now back in control.

As if in proof those smugglers who had been caught were made to line up on the quayside where they stood looking defiant despite their restraints. Around them the police and excisemen who, it has to be said, were looking murderous as they contemplated their own injuries. All of them far from forgiving which was, perhaps, understandable. After all, blood spilled even in the course of duty is still blood spilled.

It has to be admitted then that the smugglers were roughly treated as they were made ready to be marched away. Even so, in fairness to Sergeant Walters and his men, it needs to be said the abuse was mainly verbal. No actual blows were struck against the defenceless prisoners in their charge. Nevertheless, it was an ill-tempered crowd who stood ready to leave the docks that night.

Having no inclination and even less reason, both police and excisemen alike were content to remain surly, especially in their dealings with the prisoners. A state of affairs which lasted for only a short while as, long before they left the quay, a change of heart was forced on them all.

It began when a scream was heard. A single scream at first, soon joined by others. Loud, piercing, shrieks as if of souls in torment; in mortal danger more like. No-one knew where nor whom it came from.

Yet they were there. All around them. Screams of terror, echoing off the buildings, floating over the river. Anguished cries to make even the strongest shiver. Out of the fog, off the buildings, across the entire docks it seemed. The screams were everywhere. Calling for help; from Man, from God. Calling for that which never came.

It never could. Hidden by fog and night those souls were lost, beyond reach. Beyond hope.

Just as quickly as they started, they were gone. In their place there was an unnatural stillness. A quiet in which police, excisemen and criminals could only stare at each other. All of them subdued. All of them more than a little afraid of such unearthly events so that it seemed only fitting when a voice, no more than a whisper, could be heard intoning: "Deliver us from evil."

"And forgive us our trespasses," other whispers joined in, lawbreakers and law keepers alike both needing the solace of those words. "For thine is the kingdom. The power and the glory. For ever and ever. Amen."

The prayer gave them all strength as the shaken men and equally shaken prisoners marched away, both sides of the law happy to leave the scene of such Godless happenings. In their hearts neither wanting to remain in such a forlorn spot.

"Never did find the cause." Sergeant Walters looked at Doyle, his tale over. "Funny thing, though, was the way those birds behaved. Black beasts that they are."

"Ravens you mean," Doyle answered, making an easy guess.

The sergeant nodded. "All around at first," he said. "Low

51

over us. But once those screams were over there was no stopping them. Off they went, and fast too."

He stopped again, shaking his head slowly in wonderment of it all before giving Doyle one last look.

"The way they flew away you'd think the devil himself was after them."

Chapter Four

In Search of Devilry

In most places built by Man, indeed in places where the hand of Man is entirely absent, there is a marked difference between the scene they present at night and that shown during the hours of daylight. A difference not merely of vision, but more of atmosphere. In the dark even the most benign of places can take on a frightening aspect. Most likely the chief cause of this is the deeper shadows which we as a species have learnt to be wary of to such an extent that a significant proportion of our science is expended on improving the means of illumination. For many reasons, some of which we have yet to fathom and some of which we never will, we prefer the light to the dark.

A fact Doyle would have been more than happy to attest to as he stood, as best as he could figure, on the same section of quay on which had once stood the police and excisemen while they listened to the screams of those unknown lost souls on that fateful night. He, of course, was there during the day when there was at least some sunlight to dispel the shadows. Not much though, it has to be said. Even in the early afternoon, the weak November sun provided little in the way of light. It was, however, sufficient to keep any fears at bay and more than enough for the task in hand.

A task he allowed himself to forego for a moment as he stared out over the river towards the buildings he knew to be the offices of merchants, shipping companies and, as ever in this world, insurance brokers. Men of trade in other words some of whose offices were already showing lights. The better for the clerks to make money for their masters as they no doubt dreamed of setting up on their own account one day.

Away to the right, almost hidden in the gloom, stood the docks themselves, as busy as ever. To his left a broad expanse of dark river flanked by buildings which, mercifully, hid the bridge from his sight. Even during the day he had no desire to re-acquaint himself with that place of horror. The memory of it still dark.

"But soon to fade," murmured Canon Jefferies beside him, correctly guessing his thoughts.

"As you say." Doyle nodded before turning to the man with a smile that was not entirely forced. "Perhaps, though, it would be better if we gave our attention to other concerns."

The canon nodded. He too had no wish to discuss a subject for which he still held himself to blame even if Doyle had made no such accusation.

"A sound idea," he announced, almost, but not quite, hiding the relief in his voice.

As will be no surprise then the subject was forever closed. In keeping with their upbringing both men would shy away from that which disturbed them, never to speak of it again. Not for them the outpouring of emotion or any other such unmanly behaviour. They would remain stoic in the face of it all. The way it should be.

As a sign of this, and to put the matter to rest, they both turned away from the river to look instead at the warehouses. Occupied now and with many labourers at work within them they gave no indication of the dark events that had once occurred there. Indeed, even the very atmosphere of the place, industrious and ordered as it was, seemed at odds with the story as related to Doyle. The same story he, in his turn, passed on to the canon who looked about him doubtfully.

"If the good sergeant is to be believed this is where it happened," he mused. "And yet ..."

With no need to finish the sentence he looked at Doyle helplessly. There was no sign, no indication, of anything untoward. Nothing to give even the slightest clue of what had taken place, or its cause. Was this to be the end of their quest, their search over and done with before the battle was even fought?

Just as helplessly Doyle looked back at him. Nothing to be said. Perhaps they had been foolish to come, certainly foolish to hope, but what other course of action was open to them? That, at least, was the argument put forward by the canon on hearing of the events as narrated by Doyle. With nothing else to guide them they must look for a sign.

As might be guessed, their search, which the canon insisted on being a part of, was to locate the source of those fearsome screams which had so upset both police and excisemen. The sound of souls crying out as the canon described it before adding he believed them to be inextricably linked to the unearthly bridge they were looking for – the means by which the devil was able to enter this world.

In this, of course, Doyle had no reason to argue, and he was happy to accompany the canon on such an expedition. No matter where they looked, however, there was nothing to be seen that might be described as ungodly, far less anything outright devilish.

It was true the common labourers at their work were a rough-looking crew, but hardly ungodly. Not judging by the respect they afforded the canon as their paths occasionally crossed. Equally the buildings themselves, smoke-blackened as they were, seemed just as innocent. The smoke, as they knew, came from the local factories and was no sign of hell fire. So where, then, were they to look.

It was a question neither man could answer until, that is, they heard it. The croak of a raven. A single, reserved, almost apologetic croak delivered in much the same way as a manservant might request an audience with his master by way of slight cough. All done in a tone of deference and respect.

Nevertheless, it was enough. Their curiosity aroused, they looked up to see a single raven flying overhead before landing sedately on the roof of a warehouse. Soon others joined it. A few only, but a few was all that was needed.

"A storytelling?" Doyle asked of the canon.

"For those who would listen," he answered with the satisfaction clear in his voice.

As they watched, each raven would take flight, fly slowly over them, then return to its rooftop perch. Clearly this was a building to be noted. Perhaps even the origin of that which they were seeking. For sure it needed further investigation, as did the owner who by all reason would have to be involved.

"A Mr J. Arthan Esquire," the canon read from the sign which figured prominently on the wall. "Licensed for the storage of liquor and tobacco," he continued before pausing for thought. "I seem to recall hearing that name somewhere before."

With a puzzled frown he stood quietly, the memory obviously elusive. Finally, he shook his head and when that freed no thoughts he shrugged.

"It will come to me presently."

"Perhaps in a different place," Doyle told him as his face became serious. "Now it would be best we left. If this Mr Arthan is indeed involved we should not be seen paying too close attention to his premises. He would likely get to hear of it."

The sense of this being beyond dispute the canon nodded and allowed himself to be taken away. Their quest was over. A sign had been given. As shown by the way the ravens took flight shortly afterwards.

Their mission complete they left and yet not in any haphazard manner. In as much as they each flew their separate ways an observer would have noted there was one place, further along the river, where the ravens dared not go. The reason why known only to them.

The two mortal men they had guided would only receive that intelligence later, after much effort and further discoveries. Until then their ignorance of such matters would remain while they, in turn, looked elsewhere for answers in places far away from the resting place of ravens. Indeed, far removed from docks or even bridge.

Further searches there being fruitless, the canon at least elected to try a different tack, as Doyle later discovered on receipt of an invitation to a much more salubrious, and far more cultural, venue. A place, in fact, which was the very epitome of such matters. That had always been the case and no doubt always would be. A place known as the Literary and Philosophical Society.

As a slight aside the central focus for all cultural activities in any city is, of course, The Literary and Philosophical Society. That place where artistic endeavours and any such events of a cerebral nature are not only tolerated but positively encouraged. The natural home for all those of an intellectual frame of mind. Let those of lower status and aspirations have their drinking dens and music halls. For those who seek enlightenment the natural choice is the above mentioned Literary and Philosophical Society.

That being granted, what then could be said of a succession of carriages delivering their occupants to the doors of that same establishment? Surely it spoke of an order being maintained, of a certain propriety, of, perhaps, civilisation itself. How else to describe such a gathering of the rich and well-to-do at that very place?

Doyle was not disposed to answer such a question as he paused for a moment to watch the arrivals before crossing the road and walking up the stone steps to that same entrance. Tonight at least he would be among the upper echelons of the city. His companions for the evening would be those who had wealth, who had titles and some who had both. An august gathering indeed supplemented in this instance by a certain member of the clergy resplendent in his finery. This being Canon Jefferies, as could be guessed, who approached him once he had divested himself of his coat and entered the main hall.

"A fine assembly," the canon remarked by way of greeting.

"To be sure," Doyle answered, glancing about him to where those who controlled most of the city and owned most of its wealth were engaged in idle conversation with each other. "And much above my station," he murmured in afterthought.

At this the canon smiled at him fondly. "Only if such things be measured by gold," he answered softly before becoming more business-like. Gesturing towards the other occupants of the room he said, "Amongst the guests here tonight you will find a certain Jacob Arthan, magistrate and philanthropist."

"Which doubtless explains my invitation," Doyle looked steadily at him; one mystery at least now solved.

"It came to me that I had heard his name mentioned as a benefactor of certain charitable institutions. Those mostly favoured by lords and their ladies. Knowing that, it was a simple enough matter to arrange our own invitations to this gathering. As it's being held in support of one of his favoured charities I knew he would be here."

The twinkle in his eye as much as the slight smile he failed to hide suggested the canon had misused his position to obtain those invitations. For sure it would never have happened in the normal course of events. Not considering the personages there. Reason enough then for Doyle to refrain from asking.

The more so as he knew the canon would insist it was all done for the greater good. In this instance that being a chance to make the acquaintance of Jacob Arthan Esquire.

"I have already done so," the canon replied when taxed by Doyle on that very issue. "In fact I see him now. Come, let me introduce you."

So saying he lead Doyle into the company of a portly figure. A man surely approaching his fiftieth year and who had been prosperous for most of them. That much at least was signified by the bulge his waistcoat only just managed to restrain, most likely by the skill of his tailor. Certainly, physical activity or want of diet played no part as even the most casual of observers could tell. This was not a man who went without.

As to character, Doyle was soon in a position to form a judgement of his own as, after the initial introduction was complete, the canon made a quite surprising statement.

"My friend here was also my companion on the day I made an excursion in the vicinity of your premises, which I mentioned."

"That so," Arthan replied equably, much to the relief of Doyle who, as can be imagined, was somewhat taken aback at such a candid revelation. "Strange noises heard you say?" Arthan continued. "Can't say I know anything about that. Never heard of such a thing."

Spoken with, perhaps, too much conviction to be completely credible was the thought which first came to Doyle. The second being Arthan had no need to repeat to him what it could be safely assumed he had already told the canon which was an interesting consideration. In his experience such needless repetition was usually a sign of something being hidden. Reason enough to steer the conversation into safer waters he decided.

"His Grace is always looking for souls so save," he said in a manner intended to be diplomatic.

"A never-ending task in this world of ours," the canon answered wryly before adding. "As to that I see someone I must speak with. If you'll excuse me."

His deeds following his words the canon moved away leaving the two of them to talk alone.

"A good man that," Arthan told Doyle with an approving nod of his head.

"A compassionate man," Doyle agreed as together they watched the subject of their conversation buttonhole another guest.

Against a background of the violins playing in the gallery together with the chatter of the rich men and their bejewelled ladies who, it was to be hoped, were their wives it was impossible to hear what the canon was saying. At a guess it was not on matters ecclesiastical, but beyond that they could have no idea even if Arthan had already reached his own conclusion as to that.

"He'll be looking for a donation," he announced with conviction before tapping the breast of his jacket where it could be assumed his pocketbook was kept. "He's already had mine. And larger than most I dare say."

If that were really the case only the canon could know although, in a manner unintended, it enabled Doyle to form an opinion about the man. He was a braggart. That much

61

could definitely be said, but was that all there was to him? Was he just someone who loved to trumpet his own deeds, or were there other deeds he kept hidden from the laws of both God and Man? A question Doyle needed to answer without knowing where to begin, although before that could even be started Arthan had a question of his own.

"You with the church too?" he asked.

Without considering that was most likely an assumption based on the inferior quality of his tailoring Doyle laughed.

"Not at all. Some would say my profession is godless. I'm with *The Chronicle*."

"The press you say," Arthan looked at him in genuine surprise. "There's a story here fit for a newspaper you think?"

Not being prepared for such an encounter Doyle was perforce lost for an answer and could only mumble what he hoped was a suitable affirmative. After all being there under what might best be described as false pretences he could hardly reveal the truth of the matter. Certainly not to his present companion who quite fortuitously came to his aid.

With a chuckle of immense self-satisfaction he remarked, "Telling your readers what their betters are doing. That's the way of it is it?"

"We believe they should be kept informed," Doyle answered, all the while telling himself this was no lie and fervently hoping Arthan would look no further into it. The truth being he believed his readers should be informed, if not necessarily about the likes of Jacob Arthan Esquire.

As it was it appeared he need have no worries.

"Quite right," the other announced. "Give them some

ambition. That's what they need. Let them have someone deserving they can look to."

By the emphatic nature of his speech and the equally emphatic way he nodded his head while speaking this was obviously something on which the man held firm opinions. The question was, what were the exact nature of those opinions? Did he truly believe the poor should have ambitions or was it more the case, as Doyle began to suspect, he wanted them to look up to him?

"And have you done anything recently that might prompt their ambitions further?" he asked, for once knowing the reaction it would provoke.

Not anger. Not even outrage at such an intrusion into his private affairs. Instead, as Doyle rightly guessed, the man smiled broadly, his smile that of the greatest self-congratulation even though he failed to answer the question directed at him, being apparently more content to talk about himself. His favourite topic, or so it seemed.

"I lead a simple life," he began in the style of those who wished it forgotten that such simplicity was mainly due to the efforts of their serving staff. "On occasion I stay at my place here when affairs of business demand it. But in the main I have a place in the country. Wetherby Manor. You know of it?"

In answer Doyle shook his head slowly. He knew nothing of the place although he could guess it would be no mere labourer's cottage.

"Upriver, by the marshes."

Arthan seemed determined that Doyle should know of it, but when the other was able to do no more than shake his head again he dismissed it with a shrug. Doubtless believing such knowledge was not for those who only wrote for *The Chronicle*.

"I have my acres," he informed Doyle in the satisfied voice of a man trying not to show his satisfaction. "My standing in the community. I aspire to nothing more than the wish to lead a good life."

"An elegant life," Doyle added to the delight of Jacob Arthan.

"You understand me exactly," he replied.

As indeed Doyle did. It was status the man craved. His wealth merely a means to achieve it.

"But would that turn him into a scoundrel?" the canon asked of Doyle when they conferred on the matter later.

"If it provided the means to greater rank I believe so," Doyle answered.

This the canon considered for a moment.

"I hoped that by leaving you alone with him you would be able to plumb the depths of his character," he eventually told Doyle. "In that it seems you succeeded. But where to go from here?"

Where indeed. That he was in some way implicated they were ready to believe, magistrate or no, but in what way, neither could answer.

Was he simply caught up in a greater evil or, could it be, had he sold his soul to the devil?

CHAPTER FIVE

SPIRITS AND RAVENS

For those who read *The Chronicle* the next day a particular item might have caught their eye. If it did they might also have wondered as to its cause. How those few lines came to be written. If so they would have been no different from Doyle, their author.

He had at first dismissed all thought of writing any such account until, that is, a certain devilment seized him. What prompted it would always be unknown, but once the notion occurred to him he was incapable of resisting it. The idea, if it could be called that, was just too overwhelming.

So it was a few lines appeared in *The Chronicle* which read:

...at the Literary and Philosophical Society last evening, a gathering in aid of those less fortunate. Prominent among the guests, Mr Jacob Arthan, who it is understood made a substantial donation.

He expected nothing to come of it, nor would he be disappointed in that. Nothing ever could. Its sole purpose, had he been pressed to supply one, was to allay the suspicions of a possibly distrustful mind. That of the same Jacob Arthan whose name he mentioned for no other reason except one.

It amused him.

For the rest it was no more than a brief interlude of no consequence as he prepared himself for matters much weightier in nature that would be taking place on that same night. Matters at once both essential to what could only be described as his investigations and yet likely to be completely irrelevant. As to which, he would only discover later, once he left his lodgings that evening to brave the bitter weather, and bitter it was.

On that November evening the sky was clear. Bright and sharp. No cloud obscured either moon or stars both of which shone down on the city providing light, but no heat; not at such a late month in the year when the summer was far gone. Its place now taken with shivering frost and the ever present threat of snow.

It was indeed cold that night. A bitter cold where the air was fresh and the streets glistened with frost. A night where even at such an early hour ice could clearly be seen. So too the breath of those out of doors. Their reasons for being outside seemingly more pressing than any desire for warmth and comfort.

As already mentioned amongst them on that chill evening, and not by any choice of his own, Doyle had to be counted. His errand that night more a summons than an invitation. For him this was not to be a pleasant diversion spent with friends of his own choosing. Rather it was an evening spent with Madame

Clara as she attempted to contact the spirits.

Although expected it has to be admitted none of this was to his liking, for which who could blame him. After all is there any of us who would take kindly to being so manoeuvred as to be press-ganged (if press-ganged is not too strong a term) into being an unwilling participant in the schemes of another, there solely because it suited her requirements.

Further to that in this particular instance for Doyle other, darker thoughts were at work on his mind. Thoughts to which the canon would most likely not have approved although it was sure he would have understood. Considering the nature of the man he would also have forgiven just as easily and both for the same reason. He also knew what thoughts would have been afflicting Doyle. He even knew their origin.

Where once Doyle had held little belief in spirits or any such entities now he knew otherwise. After his experience on the bridge he was, if not a changed man, certainly wiser; more aware of the dark forces that perpetually surrounded this mortal world. More worrisome still he now knew how frail and vulnerable men were when confronted with these manifestations. How little they were able to resist.

So what then was he to think of a deliberate attempt to summon such beings. What also was he to think of Madame Clara. Was she a charlatan as he had at first supposed or did she indeed have some mystical power, previously unsuspected. If so to what end would it be used. Should she summon the spirits would she be able to control them as she claimed or would some malign being force its dominance over her.

Dark thoughts to be taking with him at what was just the

start of the evening, yet they were there. As much a part of this affair as the raven perched on the wall opposite the home of Madame Clara. Only one so this was to be no storytelling although one was surely enough for such a night, or so he most fervently hoped. Any more would have suggested dark deeds, or even darker beings, were afoot when he had no mood for either.

That it was there for him he had no doubt. In no other way could its attendance be explained. The more so as its eyes remained fixed on him as he walked along the avenue. Its presence signalled by a single croak whose meaning he had yet to decipher. Was it warning, rebuke or a simple statement that he was being watched over. For the life of him he would never know; not then, not ever.

A flurry of movement ahead of him caught his eye. A rustle of branches behind. More ravens arriving, finding perches where they could. Enough for a storytelling he wondered at last, then put such thoughts aside as he realised he was encircled. Around him now the ravens stood; silent, staring, but there. The comfort he had taken from the presence of only a single raven rapidly fading as more arrived, and more again. The reason for it entirely their own.

Not knowing their intent, but believing it to be benign, Doyle decided to give it no more thought. In his reasoning, if there was cause for their presence it would be made clear in time. Exactly how that might be he had no idea, his reasoning not being progressed to that extent, but he was still content to wait although in this case he had no other choice. Whoever the ravens might communicate with it was not mortal man.

He was, therefore, in complete ignorance as to their motives when he stood outside the house of Madame Clara and pulled on the bell. As he did so the air filled with the sound of beating wings. A rush of wind as collectively the ravens took silent flight. Their purpose fulfilled or thwarted he knew not, nor could he know if they left because there was no need of their presence or, perhaps, because he was beyond their help. His only thought that he was soon to find out as the door opened and he was ushered into the parlour where was waiting Madame Clara.

As might be supposed she was not alone. With her was a man, dark and slim, whose face had yet to feel the benefit of a razor that day. A shifty, suspicious looking fellow whom Doyle was instantly wary of even if Madame Clara had no such reservations.

"This is Nathaniel, my confidante and protector," she informed him before turning to another couple whom she introduced simply as the Dobsons.

The Dobsons were by their appearance the very epitome of genteel respectability. He with his whiskers well-trimmed and she with her fair hair tied back and uncomplicated. They were, it can be said, of the type that makes a goodly part of the population in any city. That is to say the faces in a crowd which can be passed without any kind of recognition or recollection.

As they informed him in all friendliness they had been attending on Madame Clara for quite some time and spoke highly of her abilities. Their evidence of this being the facility by which she was able to contact their son. An infant taken by Cholera.

To this Doyle had no ready answer and could only hope they obtained some comfort from this in however small a measure. His thoughts about the morality of what he understood to be a purely commercial transaction he kept to himself. Such business was theirs not his. Nevertheless, it was to his immense relief that their discourse was curtailed when the final guest of the evening arrived. The woman who Doyle knew to be the sister of one of those poor unfortunates who had perished at the bridge.

What can be said of the woman who now walked in? What can any man say on first meeting the woman who would one day be his wife? Doyle, for sure, had no answer other than she was captivating.

Her blonde hair was long, neatly tied with ribbon. Her smile at once both open and friendly. Even her very poise seemed designed to enchant him. Beyond doubt he was smitten and eager to make her acquaintance. For which service he turned to Madame Clara who kept him waiting no longer.

"Allow me to present Miss Clarice Burton," she said, her shrewd eyes missing nothing. "And this is the gentleman I mentioned. Mr Ignatius Doyle of *The Chronicle*," she continued, turning to the woman just named.

"My condolences on the loss of your brother," Doyle murmured as he held her slim hand for longer than was, perhaps, strictly proper.

"My thanks," she answered him. "It came as a shock to us all. Particularly as he gave no indication of any troubles."

"For which we are here seeking explanations," Madame Clara announced briskly, anxious to make it clear her services were mystical rather than matrimonial in nature.

"Indeed," the man known as Nathaniel joined in, his voice deep and low. "Everything has been prepared."

By this, of course, he meant all preparations had been made for an attempt to contact the spirits as they saw for themselves when Madame Clara lead them into an adjoining room where seats had been arranged around a table. Four were of the sort that would be expected to be found in any respectable dining room. One was of a much sturdier construction with the last being the most elaborate of all. High backed and with wide arms it was decorated with intricate carvings showing, as far as could be ascertained in the dim light, the signs of the zodiac interspersed with a variety of flora. This, as there was no need of saying, was for Madame Clara.

Guided by her they each took their seats. The Dobsons sat together, after which it was arranged that Doyle should sit next to Miss Burton. Whether this was for mystical reasons or because Madame Clara was not above playing matchmaker they could never know. Nevertheless, they sat together with Nathaniel taking the sturdier chair by the side of Madame Clara.

Alone amongst them she remained standing as they each took their seats. Then, bidding them to remain silent she placed a hand bell in the centre of the bare table.

"So the spirits can announce their presence," she told them while carefully placing a glass jar over it. "So it can be rung only by the spirits," she then whispered.

Finally a candle was lit. Its light was sufficient to show her as she extinguished the gas lamps, leaving it the only source of illumination. With thick drapes covering the windows all was now darkness save for that single flame; a flickering oasis of light in which their faces were only just visible.

Taking her seat now she had them all hold hands. A second or two she waited, then she spoke in a voice hushed and reverential.

"You must all remain quiet," she all but breathed. "The spirits are shy creatures who are easily disturbed. Should that happen they will leave never to return this evening. Nor, I might add, do they enjoy the light. We must wait for their arrival in darkness."

So saying she blew out the candle. The room now plunged into stygian blackness and silence. To be seen, nothing. To be heard, nothing.

In darkness now they waited. Each to their own thoughts, or their own fears. Madame Clara aside no-one could say what would happen next, or indeed if anything would happen on this occasion. For that they could only wait either for prayers to be answered, or fears realised.

The darkness was oppressive in its stillness. A deep breath, as if a sigh, now and then heard. Together, yet isolated, they sat, waiting and then waiting more. The night not theirs they each sat alone with their thoughts until, at last, it happened.

The bell rang.

Twice. No more. Then all was quiet again, unless gasps of surprise or consternation be counted. For sure nothing else disturbed the darkness in which they all sat, hands tightly clasped, as that single tone died away. Its absence worse than its presence.

All was apprehension now. A tension into which Madame Clara spoke softly, almost soothingly.

"A spirit is amongst us. We mean it no harm as it means no harm to us. In peace and goodwill we ask only that it speaks to those it left behind for which I offer myself as its medium."

At that she fell silent. Waiting for an answer, perhaps, or biding her time. Only she knew, unless spirits were indeed amongst them. Their presence yet to be announced.

Afraid, they waited, not knowing who would speak or what would be said. Not even knowing which one of them would be spoken to, or why. All of them at a loss until, in the darkness, the table moved.

It rose. It fell. It rose again, turning as it did so. Back to the floor it crashed. One side tilted, then the other, the table rocking violently. Again it rose high. Again it dropped back to the floor. Then it lay still; moving no more. All fury spent it became immobile, inert, giving no indication of what it signified, or what would happen next. Those present could only wait in fear and apprehension.

Bound together more by fright than clasped hands they were each one helpless. Lost to the events as they unfolded. Neither actor nor willing participant they could only follow where another lead. Their guide in this, Madame Clara spoke again.

"The spirit amongst us is troubled. Perhaps its passing was not easy. It seeks answers of its own for which we must be ready to help. Spirit I beseech you be calm. Speak to us through the frail body I again offer to you so that you may find peace."

As she finished there was silence for but seconds. A silence in which they dared neither move nor speak. Even their very breath seemed frozen within them as they waited for the spirit to give voice. Words that never came.

In its stead the wild screech of a raven.

Clearly heard it called out. Its call sharp and loud, almost angry. A call repeated as others joined in. Their calls equally harsh. From every window now it came. The screeches of ravens pouring out their anger and their scorn.

Too loud to be ignored. Too wild to be dismissed. The sheer cacophony such an assault on their senses they were forced to take notice. Even Madame Clara found she had no choice other than to abandon all thoughts of speaking with the spirits. Such communication being impossible under the circumstances as she was forced to accept, but with a very ill grace.

Striking a vesta she lit the candle by whose light all could now be seen. The faces of those around her telling their own mute tale. Being so far outside their expectations they could do no more than stare at her as if in some way she was responsible. As if her attempts to summon the spirits had upset the elemental forces of nature itself.

In reply she opened her mouth to speak only to find speech impossible over the continuing screech of the ravens. As alternative she shook her head only to find that equally ineffectual. Accusing eyes still looked at her making it clear they thought she was the culprit.

At this her temper snapped. All patience gone. She was in charge of these proceedings, the ravens merely interlopers.

Matching the action to her thoughts she jumped up from

her seat, angrily striding towards a window. There she snapped the drapes back seemingly intent of confronting those same creatures. Those challengers to her authority she would face down; make them account for their actions.

As she did so, standing at the window with its drapes wide apart, she plainly believed herself to be in charge. The ravens naught but birds. She believed her will would prevail. An opinion she was soon to find sorely tested.

No sooner were the drapes flung back than a raven appeared. Wings outstretched, eyes blazing, it glared at her. Its screech rising above the others, sharp and loud. She was the intruder it seemed to say. She was the one meddling in their affairs.

At sight of it she stepped back. A cry of fright on her lips. She staggered, she swooned. She would have fallen had not Nathaniel rushed to her side. His arms supporting her as she cowered away from the vision at the window.

Doyle, meanwhile, had also risen, his steps taking him to the gas lamps which were soon lit. Their light doing much to dispel the, can it be said, dark mood which had settled around them. With shadows gone so too were the primeval fears that oft come in their wake. The result being far more wholesome.

It was also by this same light that Doyle noticed something no doubt Madame Clara would have wished to remain hidden. Certainly she would have been hard pressed to find an adequate explanation. That was not to say such a thing was lacking. Perhaps the reason was perfectly innocent. Only Madame Clare could say for sure. Until then, however, Doyle had cause to wonder at the hand bell, identical to that still under its glass jar on the table, which he saw lying by the side of her chair. Which one had really rung, he asked of himself, and was it done by spirit or human hand? So too with the table. Whose hand had really moved it?

Doyle already knew the answer and with that understanding came a release such as he had never felt before. No spirits had been involved that night meaning his darkest forebodings were unrealised. There was no danger of him again having to face the dark entity he had encountered on the bridge. Nor would Miss Burton and with that knowledge came an immense happiness. So much so he was almost ready to forgive Madame Clara and allow her play acting to continue.

That it did there was no doubt. Perhaps because they recognised him or for some other entirely separate reason as Doyle turned up the lights the ravens at first fell quiet, then disappeared completely. Now, in the silence and the light, Madame Clara was able to compose herself.

"The spirits are disturbed tonight. More than I've ever witnessed before," she said, the tremor in her voice entirely genuine.

"It was brave of you to still offer yourself as their host," Nathaniel told her in a voice whose solicitude was either more play acting or also genuine. Doyle could not be certain. "Who knows what might have happened had you become possessed."

In acknowledgement of this Madame Clara bowed her head modestly.

"We must all do what we can for those who are troubled," she said, equally modestly. "My gifts must always be at their disposal or else why was I given them."

Doyle had to admit it was a pretty speech, well delivered. Also effective in that it allowed her to assume control once more and lead them back into the parlour after announcing the spirits would not be returning that night.

"But what of the birds?" Miss Burton asked of her.

"The ravens," Doyle added.

"What indeed," Madame Clara answered. "By long tradition they appear only when some calamity is about to happen which makes me fear greatly for the future," she shook her head. "Who knows what is about to befall us."

After this, the Dobsons soon left. Madame Clara personally saw them to the door so that Doyle would never know if any remuneration had taken place or indeed if any other arrangements had been made. That being no business of his.

Now in their absence she could only confess herself to be at a loss and completely exhausted. Exhaustion being the usual result of communing with the spirits according to the still present Nathaniel. How much of this was more play acting Doyle had no way of knowing although on this occasion at least he was prepared to believe it was genuine. His proof being the fact that never once did she think to ask him what he intended to write in *The Chronicle*.

Of more immediate relevance as she was, and looked, exhausted there could be no further value in any conversation with her. Neither her thoughts nor her words were likely to be intelligible. Reason enough to take their leave of her which was done with little ceremony.

For reasons of more than just gallantry Doyle insisted on seeing Miss Burton safely home and took delight in her ready agreement. Modestly he accepted she may have just felt in need of some masculine company after the frights of the evening, but he could still hope something of a more intimate nature was involved. At the very least he would have her company for a little longer which was sufficient for the moment. Certainly he could ask for no more as they started their journey home; intending to walk to the nearby high street, there to hail a passing cab.

By this time, the avenue was white with frost. Thick and hard it clung to the bare branches of the trees and crackled under their boots. Everywhere that evening had a white coating. A veil against which the black of the ravens stood out in sharp relief.

They had returned. Their purpose still unknown. Their mood impossible to judge, but they were there; more and more of them.

Silently arriving they flew overhead, circling slowly. As they did so something fell from their beaks to fall gently around the two humans now standing still if only out of surprise. That this was of import neither of them doubted even if the significance of it all was still vague. Not even Doyle with his recently acquired, nay hard earned, experience could penetrate the mind of the ravens. So it was neither could fathom why slivers of green should be falling around them, nor even what they might be.

For her part Miss Burton bent down to pick up one such sliver so she could examine it more closely.

"It appears to be marsh grass," she decided once her inspection was complete. Then, by way of explanation, she added, "I have an interest in Botany."

Of course she would have an interest in such things Doyle thought, still unable to see the significance until, that is, the memory of a previous evening came back to him. In his remembrance Jacob Arthan had told him of his home by the marshes. The same marshes to which it seemed the ravens were now indicating. Their intention was suddenly clear.

Seeking confirmation Doyle also picked up a green token, for which it really was, and looked towards the sky. More precisely, he looked towards the ravens now perched on bare branches to see them looking back at him as if waiting for a sign. A sign from him. It was his acknowledgement they were waiting for so that once he nodded in acceptance of their message they were able to leave.

By what mysterious means they communicated with each other would never be known, but communicate they did. Once Doyle nodded in understanding they took flight as one. Their job done. Doyle now knew where to look for further answers and all thanks entirely to the ravens.

Their storytelling continued.

Chapter Six

A Gruesome Discovery

In any gentleman worthy of the name, there will always be a sense of honour. For such as these the keeping of a word will be more than just a duty, nor yet an obligation. It will be such an essential part of their self that to break it would be unthinkable. No matter if it be bound by contract, by handshake or just simple promise the result would always be the same. A word given was a word kept.

This was the position in which Doyle now found himself. Having given his word to Madame Clara, admittedly under what might be described as Force Majeure, he was now honour bound to write an account of the previous evening for *The Chronicle*. While it was true he could have mentioned the second hand bell, perhaps even speculated as to its function, and informed his readers the only reply came from the ravens that was not, he felt, within the intention of the agreement. Within its spirit as humourists might say.

As he well knew Madame Clara desired an article that would extol her talents as a mystic. An account of her capacity to summon the spirits although that she signally failed to do on the evening in question. And therein lay the problem. How could Doyle in all conscience keep his word to Madame Clara while maintaining the integrity of *The Chronicle*? The two surely were incompatible.

This was the conundrum he had to resolve which could only be done, as he decided after much thought, by a simple statement of such facts as would compromise neither his integrity nor his honour. For which reason all those who read *The Chronicle* that next day would have seen the following:

At the home of the mystic Madame Clara last evening an attempt was made to contact the spirits of those departed only for it to be interrupted by ravens, the cause of this being unknown. It is noted, however, that ravens have always appeared when a tragedy is imminent making Madame Clara fear for the future. No doubt she will attempt to contact the spirits again to request their help in this matter.

In the opinion of Doyle at least this kept his pledge to Madame Clara while not carrying any outright falsehoods. Should she feel otherwise, of course, his defence would be that he had only agreed to write about such events as actually happened. She could ask no more of him than that.

Equally so he could pride himself in the knowledge that he committed no dishonour on the night he also met Miss Burton. Perhaps that was of importance only to himself although he dared to hope she too would appreciate it. As far as he was concerned her opinion of him was as important as his honour.

For sure he wished to be trusted by more than just ravens. As with any man who valued his honour, his integrity, he wished it to be known to others. He wished, in fact, for his word to be taken on trust, and not just by ravens.

As to that, of course, he could only assume he had their trust. A thought, unbidden yet insistent, suggested they trusted him no more than he might trust a well-trained lap dog. A creature who would do as it was told without thought of its own simply because a command had been given. In his case – the command (or was it just a suggestion?) that he should visit the country that lay beyond the confines of the city. He should, in fact, visit the marshes. More than that he should do it soon no matter what the weather.

While it was true that with flecks of snow falling from a dark sky which threatened more it was no time to visit the countryside. True also it was no time even to be out of doors unless duty or employment dictated otherwise. On such a freezing day those more accustomed to the shelter and comfort of a city should not have ventured so far abroad as to be outside its confines where open fields offered no respite from the cold and hedgerows little shelter from the biting wind. People such as these would have been better advised to stay at home and wait until summer arrived.

Then they would have seen the countryside at its finest. Its blues and greens and golds as a myriad of flowers opened themselves to the sun while brightly coloured butterflies danced overhead. All of them rejoicing in the very fact of being alive at such a glorious time. Truly that was a sight to lift the spirits and gladden the soul of even the most curmudgeonly.

A time of peace and tranquillity far removed from the barren wasteland of that November scene.

From this, then, it can be assumed that those present on such a bleak morning were there not by choice. A calling of some kind must have brought them to that very spot which, it should be said, was a correct assumption although not as far as the matter of choice was concerned. Here two of the individuals accepted that such an expedition was necessary and made a positive choice to do it despite the wintry conditions while the third individual insisted she should accompany them. The two in question being, as should need no telling, Doyle and Canon Jefferies with the third being Miss Burton, also as could be guessed.

That being said her presence, perhaps, requires some explanation. It being not immediately obvious why she might have been there nor what she might know of ravens whose trail they were now so earnestly following. In which case the story must be told.

The beginning of it was, of course, that very same night when Miss Burton exercised what might be described as her feminine prerogative to ask of Doyle the true purpose of the ravens. Having noticed he seemed neither surprised nor alarmed by their gift, naturally she wanted to know more. Unfortunately for Doyle these were questions for which he had no answer. Certainly none he was prepared to share with a lady such as her. However, as is so often the case with members of her gender, her curiosity would not be satisfied until Doyle could do no more than suggest they met with Canon Jefferies.

The tale, he judged, would be better told by a member of the clergy.

By fortunate chance, if that be an appropriate term, Miss Burton already knew the canon as he had officiated at the funeral of her brother so there was little need of introduction on either side. The canon also remembered Miss Burton. A happy fact which meant the conversation could almost immediately progress to the cause of their visit.

As befits a man of the cloth, not to mention his infinitely forgiving nature, the canon did no more than raise a quizzical eyebrow when he heard of their evening with Madame Clara. His religion and his conviction apparently proof against any such irregular activities. Nevertheless, he was plainly concerned when the ravens were mentioned. His face being so obviously troubled that Miss Burton felt compelled to ask the reason why. An answer the canon eventually gave. It was not done lightly, nor was the answer immediate. At first the canon paused to reflect, possibly even to pray, then he told her all.

To her credit Miss Burton took the story calmly, even serenely, a smile of satisfaction slowly appearing on her face.

"So my brother didn't die by his own hand," she murmured. "That thought has caused me much pain. But now my mind can be at rest for which I thank you. I thank you both."

Spoken with such gratitude no man could have remained unmoved by her words, the canon in particular nodding his own appreciation in return. His had been a difficult decision, taken in the hope it would give her some comfort. Now, seeing that was indeed the case, he could be satisfied his judgement had been sound.

Doyle, meanwhile, had sat quietly, taking no part in this conversation until she turned towards him.

"And I especially thank you for enduring so much in the discovery of this," she told him, daring to lay a tender hand on his arm. "Your gallantry on the bridge speaks much to your character."

In as much as he was happy to bask in such praise Doyle nevertheless felt constrained to deny his part in any of this, as a gentleman should.

"I was given much in the way of assistance," he mumbled.

"No doubt because your first thought was to save another," she answered with the softest of smiles. "Such an action deserved to be rewarded."

Was it because of the gentleness of her nature that she saw this so clearly? Doyle would never know, nor, it has to be said, would the canon, neither of them having considered the matter before her answer came as something of a surprise to them both. Now, of course, they were prepared to believe the truth had been revealed through her and with that thought came an overwhelming sense of security. They were not alone. Another, higher being was protecting them as they, in turn, attempted to do His work.

"We may win through yet," the canon breathed, quite forgetting himself.

"But first we must interpret the message," Doyle reminded him, having a more practical turn of mind. "My thoughts are it refers to the marshes where Arthan has his home. Wetherby Manor as I recall."

His thoughts returning from what might be described as

a higher plane, the canon agreed on that with little hesitation. Indeed, as he remarked why else would the ravens present them with what Miss Burton had already identified as marsh grass unless they intended such a sign to be followed. That being so obvious they resolved there and then to go, no matter the weather. Even if they had no inkling as to what they might find, as the canon also remarked, they would at least go with hope.

A sentiment with which they did indeed travel although, as the observant reader will have remembered, on this occasion Doyle and the canon were accompanied by Miss Burton. In this it can be correctly assumed the arrangement was not to the immediate liking of the two men concerned, the thought of any danger being enough to raise their protests. To this Miss Burton countered by saying no real danger was envisaged. Furthermore, as she also said, her connection to these events was of a far more intimate and personal nature than theirs, giving her the right to be involved. The sense, and the justice, of this being so clear that eventually an agreement was reached. Their final objection was overcome by the thought that with the canon present to act as chaperone she need fear no damage to her reputation.

So with her honour as a lady intact and their honour as gentlemen equally confirmed an expedition was duly made to the countryside in which this narrative began. That cold and misty place where they now found themselves. Their boots left no mark on the hard, frozen ground beneath them.

Indeed, more than just the rough track they were walking along was frozen that day. The entire world it seemed was covered in a mantle of frost and shrouded in an early morning mist through which the sun shone only palely; its weak, watery, beams barely sufficient to show them the road ahead. Their starting point was already lost behind a white veil.

Such then were the conditions under which they laboured; each step taking them further along the track and yet seemingly no further towards any resolution of this mystery, for mystery it was. With little to guide them save a few blades of grass they could have no idea where they should be looking or what they should be looking for. Their only hope being that when they saw it they would understand.

A vague and in many ways unsatisfactory state of affairs were made all the worse when the track they were following came to an end. In front of them now, as much as they could see anything in front of them, was nothing more than open moorland. Their way no longer clearly marked. Their path suddenly unknown.

A fact which, as might be expected, caused a brief discussion after which it was agreed they should strike out at an angle in the general direction of the river and the marshes surrounding it. There, it was hoped, they would find their answer whatever it might be. Hardly a brilliant strategy as they had to admit, but it was at least a course of action when they had no other. That being said its major flaw, as they soon discovered, was the mist all around them.

After no more than few score yards they stopped to look around them and to take stock.

"The very gates of Hell itself could be over yonder hill and we could walk past them without knowing," the canon muttered, staring into the distance as if that alone would clear the mist.

His words were true and yet, surprisingly Doyle refused to share in the general pessimism, smiling slightly instead. His words when he answered were confident.

"I think we would be best served to wait here."

Seeking explanation they turned to him, but he merely shook his head before looking towards the sky. He was waiting for something. Exactly what only he could know until, that is, they arrived.

As if summoned black shapes appeared through the mist. Ravens. Flying low, swooping and circling around the three who could only stand and marvel.

"Another storytelling," the canon murmured with an admiring glance at Doyle. "You knew."

"I guessed," he answered.

His statement was true in the main although, perhaps, not entirely accurate. Far from a guess it was more of a feeling, an intuition. Without even being aware of the process involved he knew the ravens would arrive, as they did. Now all that remained was to interpret their meaning.

A task made simple by the ravens themselves. Their circling at an end they all headed off in the same direction to make their intention an easy guess. That was the course to be taken. In no other way could such behaviour be construed.

Accordingly, then, they allowed themselves to be guided for at least part of the way, anything else being impossible. The low lying mist saw to that by obscuring their view of the birds once they flew no more than a few yards away. Even so once they began the next stage of their journey under watchful eyes the ravens seemed content they had been understood and vanished completely. Presumably they felt the mortal humans beneath them could be trusted with the simple task of walking.

Perhaps in fairness to those same people it should be said they in their turn trusted the ravens not to abandon them at such a point. More than that it was not even considered so, even when the ravens disappeared completely, they had no hesitation in walking on. Noting as they did so their steps were taking them ever closer to the marsh whose grass had meant so much to the ravens. Proof enough they were being guided correctly even if, as yet, they had no idea where those steps would take them.

Eventually they reached what to call a path would be an exaggeration. A track beaten down by many boots would be a better description. It allowed them to walk in single file only as the grass and the bracken closed in around them. The undergrowth soon reached above their heads until their walk was through a dark green corridor of vegetation, close and dripping wet.

Who could have made such a path and why were questions unanswered. That it had been made was all they could know as, step by step, the path was trod. Not happily, surely no-one would willingly do that, but still it was done. They had come too far to turn back now.

For reasons of gender and age Doyle took the lead with Miss Burton behind him and the canon bringing up the rear. In which fashion they moved on, going steadily deeper into that strange underworld. That place where all sounds, all words, were muffled; where the air itself was stale and musty. That place where evil could flourish, where dark deeds must have already taken place. Why else would the ravens bring them there.

Why indeed and when would they find out. Thoughts which occupied them all as they toiled through the green oppression with its foul smelling atmosphere. Surely they would know soon and surely they did. From out of the mist, somewhere ahead, came the sound they should have expected. The harsh croak of a raven.

A summons. A warning. Neither or both, how could they know. It was not the soft tone with which the canon was usually favoured or the screech with which they had treat Madame Clara. It was somewhere in between. An instruction perhaps. A message certainly, but to what end.

Even while that was still unknown a foreboding began to fill them. A sense of dread at what was to come.

"Not for nothing do the ravens call," the canon muttered as they stopped at the sound of it, unsure what their next actions should be.

"True words," Doyle answered grimly as the statement, spoken plainly, helped him reach a decision. "It might be best if you stayed here," he continued, putting that decision into words. "Let me go on alone to see what there is to be seen."

In his eyes a sensible suggestion. The correct decision under the circumstances he felt which is not to say there was universal accord. The canon for sure was not happy that he might once again be putting Doyle in jeopardy. The guilt he still held from that previous encounter on the bridge still hanging heavy. Even so, albeit with much reluctance, he agreed; telling Doyle to go with God. As for Miss Burton, although concern showed plainly on her face, she kept to her position in life and raised no argument. Not yet being his wife she could do no more.

An arrangement which allowed Doyle to do as he first proposed and head further down the path on his own. That was not to say he was in any way happy about this, far from it, but at least he could be sure no-one else was walking into danger and for him that was more than sufficient. The danger he himself might have to face but a small price to pay assuming, of course, he would be in any danger. Usually the ravens had warned him if he was taking the wrong path, even if he had not always listened, so who could say they would steer him wrong now when they seemed to be positively inviting his presence.

More than that they were actually guiding him along. Ravens now on both sides of him. Their soft calls provided encouragement rather than warning as he forced his way through the ever thickening undergrowth. His target, and he destination, one single clear raven call.

Louder than the rest it was the beacon he followed. His sole guide as he stumbled through a tangle of reeds and grasses tall enough to hide everything else from sight. Tall enough even so that his entire world consisted of nothing more than the green, and occasional brown, of the vegetation around which floated the calls of his avian guides. Their voices alone keeping him from going astray as he stumbled, slid, staggered forward until at last he was there. His destination reached.

Not that he knew it immediately. His first thought was mainly relief at no longer being in that green entanglement when he finally burst through it to find himself in what could best be described as a clearing. It was only later, after he took a deep breath of fresh air, that he looked around to find he was by the edge of the marsh. By the edge of water certainly, a thin film of ice over it.

This scene was suddenly interrupted by the harsh call of the ravens. All of them calling loudly as they took to the air around him. The sky full with them as he turned this way and that desperate to make sense of their flight and their calls. Even more was he desperate to discover their purpose in bringing him to such a spot. There had to be a reason.

As ever the ravens had guided him right. Confirmed as it was by his discovery of that which they intended him to find. The reason why he was there now clearly visible, yet horrible to behold.

Poking through the ice were two arms, human arms, hands reaching upwards as if in prayer. Limbs perhaps muscular once, but now desiccated by cold reaching up out of the ice which obscured whatever lay beneath. The mortal remains of some unknown beyond doubt, but seeking what. Was it mercy, forgiveness or benediction that had been the last request of this lost soul.

At first Doyle could only stare, transfixed. Surely not another poor soul taken by the darkness, but if not then what did it signify. Who had met their end in such a cold and lonely way.

Answers Doyle determined to discover as he carefully stepped by the edge of the water. Not too close lest he miss his step and fall in, but close enough to soon bring him to that ghastly sight. The very thing he had come to find now the very thing he wished he could avoid. If only that were possible. If only he knew how.

Instead, and setting all such qualms aside, he steeled himself to look further. To take one last step towards the ice so he could peer through it. The task which he knew was his alone.

A face stared up at him, lips drawn back in a rictus of terror. Proof, if proof be needed, that this had been no easy end. This was a death marked by violence, by malice. The wanton disposal of the corpse signifying that and more.

At the sight Doyle pulled back, stumbled, almost fell, only just maintaining his balance on that icy embankment. His breath hard, deep, as he struggled to retain his equilibrium. At first capable of doing no more than stare in horror at so gruesome a sight. He could only stand and wait. The cold air clearing his head so comprehension could return.

That was when he looked towards the sky to see the ravens leaving. Their mission, or their storytelling, concluded, they had no further part to play in all of this. Whatever happened now belonged entirely in the realm of Man, for the time being at least.

Chapter Seven

Of The Bridge

What can be said of the bridge. That bridge. The bridge still dark in Doyle's memory, and with good reason. There was no artistic merit to its appearance nor had any been intended. In form it was purely functional. A means for the river to be crossed at a place convenient for those who built it.

There were, perhaps, those of an artistic temperament who could look at the bridge, at the river and the city around them both, and find a certain beauty in it all. If so this particular night was for them. With clouds only partially covering the moon, its beams reflected off the river so that it shone out in silver against which the bridge stood in silent silhouette. Truly a night where an artist could find beauty, tranquillity even.

So it was to his misfortune that Doyle would never be numbered amongst those. His had always been the view of the pragmatist. The seeker of truth not beauty. For him, therefore, the bridge was simply a construction. His purpose for being there that night was not to admire it, nor even to cross it if that could be avoided. He was there for another reason. As was the figure who he knew would be keeping a lonely vigil there and not just for this night. If he was right it had been done for several nights preceding this.

How many he could only guess and certainly had no intention of asking. That night he was not there to gather information. He was there to perform what he hoped would be taken as a kindly act. A necessary act for sure even if it might not be appreciated as such by the lone figure he had just spotted half hidden in the shadows. The very person he had come to comfort so their twin motives for being there could be reconciled.

"A cold night," he began as he approached the figure.

At this the other gave a start. Too engrossed in staring at the bridge he had failed to notice Doyle quietly walking towards him. Failed even to hear the footsteps. Now in surprise he stepped out of the shadows so moonlight and gas light together could reveal him to be Canon Jefferies.

"You, here," he stuttered. He could think of nothing else to say.

"But not for the same reason as you," Doyle told him; the look on his face alone showing he thought he knew why the canon had been conducting such a cold and lonely vigil.

That needed no telling. On hearing the tale from Doyle he had taken it upon himself to mount guard over the bridge. Night after night standing there, ready to intervene if the darkness returned seeking fresh victims. Ready, no doubt, to risk his very soul should that be called for. Doyle knew it as certainly as if the canon had made him his confessor.

"How could you know?" he asked, stealing a glance towards the sky as if he believed it had been a message from the ravens.

Seeing this Doyle smiled slightly. "It was your own behaviour today that told me the most of it," he replied.

At this point it should be said their conversation was taking place on the evening of the day they had visited the marshes. It was, therefore, those events to which Doyle was referring. More exactly he meant their grisly find and all subsequent activities.

The story of these properly begins when Doyle returned to Miss Burton and the canon with news of his discovery. That he had indeed found something they had already guessed from the sudden departure of the ravens. Now that was confirmed, and they were made aware of the exact nature of the discovery, a suitable course of action needed to be agreed. A discussion in which, as Doyle noted, the canon took very little part. He seemed pre-occupied, withdrawn even, so any decisions as were taken almost passed him by.

At least that was the assumption until, by mutual agreement, Doyle and Miss Burton made to leave. It was then the canon roused himself, agreeing they should go, but also insisting he should stay. His place, as he declared, was with the departed whose soul needed tending. An opinion on which he held firm.

Accordingly, then, Doyle and Miss Burton left him to his prayers while they went to inform the authorities. Even if his soul was in good hands his body still remained in the mortal world where its death would have to be recorded and most likely investigated. A process which, of course, could only begin once it had been recovered from its current location for which many strong hands would be required. In short the constabulary were called for.

It was their grim duty to lift that frozen body from its ice-covered resting place and transport it elsewhere. After which those who had found it were asked to explain the exact circumstances of its finding. A botanical expedition as had already been agreed would be their story with no mention of ravens. That would have been asking too much of the stolid officials now in charge of what had been described as the investigation. Fortunately, however, the presence of the canon was enough to give their fiction sufficient reliability for it to remain unquestioned.

Even so, a good many hours passed before they were free to return home. A long journey in its own right during which, as Doyle noticed, the canon seemed anxious, as if he was expected elsewhere.

"You constantly looked at the sky not your Hunter, your watch, so it couldn't be an appointment at some agreed time which concerned you," Doyle told him. "Then I realised it was the coming darkness which was the cause of your unease."

"So you guessed I would be here," the canon said with an air of sullen defeat.

"Not at first," Doyle answered, giving the man a curious look. His attitude held a puzzle. "But then I talked to your church warden who said you had taken to going out every evening. Visiting parishioners you claimed. That was when I made the guess."

"A good one too," the canon replied with only a slight glance towards him. "But it fails to explain why you came after me."

"Because you cannot do this every night," Doyle told him softly, concern for the wellbeing of the man evident in his voice.

"Except I must.".

He said no more. He had no need to say more. They both knew he would never allow some innocent soul to walk into danger on that bridge. He would give up his own life before that would happen. For sure his own health he would deem a small price to pay.

"Then what we must do, the two of us, is find another way," Doyle told him expecting a reply, an acknowledgement at least, yet receiving none. Once again the canon seemed content to remain passive.

"Perhaps if we asked the police to patrol here," Doyle continued, being forced to speak by the silence of the other. "Two police constables, strong-minded men, would surely be more than a match for any harmful forces that might come by."

This the canon seemed to think about. The thoughtful look that appeared on his face certainly gave that impression.

"But would the police agree to it?" he asked, his face now clearing.

"If a man in your position were to mention his concerns about the likelihood of others taking their lives here how could they refuse?" Doyle replied before adding with a grin, "And I'm sure *The Chronicle* would print a word or two on the subject."

Finally the canon chuckled. Only slightly to be sure, but at least his dark mood seemed to be lifting.

"And for tonight?" he asked, this time feeling able to look at Doyle.

"That we will do together."

It would be a cold duty, waiting there until the hour progressed sufficiently so they could be sure no-one was likely to come along. Nevertheless, it would be done. They would both stay there with Doyle at least wondering if the recent lack of fatalities was due to the presence of the canon and the crucifix he could now see the man holding.

He hoped it was so. That way the canon could feel he had done some good which, Doyle felt, would help to calm his soul.

The man deserved that and so much more. Indeed, he had taken the whole of this matter onto himself from the outset which, while demonstrating a compassion even few of the clergy could equal, was nonetheless to the detriment of his health, possibly also to his soul. No mortal man could accept so much of the suffering of others, something the canon well knew despite letting it pass disregarded at least until a suitable alternative could be found. The alternative now suggested by Doyle who had grown too fond of the canon to allow his continued suffering.

It was in that vein that he was happy to offer the services of *The Chronicle* despite what some might see as a contradiction. After all, for a newspaper to report on the works of Man was nothing out of the ordinary. For the same newspaper to report on the misdeeds of Man was in every way a routine event. A sad fact it may be, but it has to be admitted that in this world of ours there will always be more miscreants than there is space in any newspaper to report their crimes. To which must be added the equally sad fact that it was the reporting of their activities which sold newspapers. Apparently everyone had an enduring fascination for these matters.

A state of affairs which, while sometimes difficult to explain, was at least understood by Doyle. It was how he earned his living. By that and the occasional story of buildings constructed or exhibitions opened. Everything that made up the life of the city as it could be described.

For all of this he was prepared, practised some might say. It was a daily occurrence, but not so the words he was now trying to find. Words that would motivate the police and help the canon which was a strange circumstance in its own right. Not often did the press find itself in the service of the church. Nevertheless, this he had committed himself to do so, after due thought, the following appeared in *The Chronicle*:

Of late a worrying trend has appeared concerning the bridge which for many years has spanned the river running through this city. Although built for commerce, in which it has performed a sterling service, it has recently been the site of several tragic events. Viz. a number of deaths have occurred there.

While there can be no doubt these were all accidental in nature the quantity of such incidents is now provoking concern. The church in particular, it is understood, has recently started to take an interest with a view to preventing further tragedies. As much as this is to be welcomed it cannot surely be the church's charge alone. In this all responsible citizens must take a part.

How that might be achieved will naturally be a matter of some debate although there can be no question this needs to be resolved. However, until that happens can it be agreed that this is a matter

with which the police should be involved. Constables posted at the
bridge would be a service greatly valued by all.

How effective such words might be Doyle would never know. After all the church, in the guise of the canon, would always have more authority than the press. At best his would be a supportive role, but it was still a part he was happy to play. If nothing else it meant he had kept his word to the canon who he knew would appreciate it.

More than that in some small measure it might help to soothe whatever it was that ailed him. Even if its cause could only vaguely be guessed at and its cure possibly beyond the powers of Man still it was there, clear to all. The soul of the canon was anguished. For reasons so far unexplained the man was troubled in ways that were obviously taking their toll on him.

With the signs of strain clearly visible Doyle could only hope he found either the cure or at least the strength to overcome it. If not what hope was there for him. Indeed, what hope was there for their quest which continued to progress albeit in ways unexpected.

Their recent discovery being a case in point. Even without knowing why they had been sent to the marshes, for that is exactly what the ravens had done, their discovery had been beyond the guess of them all. Now all they could do was seek the help of those qualified to give it and hope it would be enough to further their cause. To help them better understand so they might overcome whatever devilry was the root cause of it all.

Reason enough to explain why they were in the mortuary again. Doctor Stanhope still no better disposed toward Doyle despite the moderating influence of Canon Jefferies.

In every other respect save one the setting was no different from their previous encounter. The lighting just as dim. The shadows just as thick and the sound just as cushioned. Everything identical except, on this occasion, the ravens were absent.

Strangely no-one missed them, not even Doyle. No-one even thought to question their absence, or what it could mean. Since neither Canon Jefferies nor Doyle would have considered the storytelling to be over, had they been asked, the ravens must surely still have a part to play. On that there could be no argument.

Perhaps this was because their attention was elsewhere. Most notably on Doctor Stanhope who looked at them both together, but kept any thoughts he might have to himself.

"Not drowned this time," he told them, keeping the conversation purely practical. "It was a knife that did for this one. A large one too, possibly even a sword."

"A violent end," the canon replied in sad tones.

At that he slid into his own thoughts, falling silent in the process and so leaving Doyle to take up the conversation.

"Is there anything more you can tell us?" he asked.

A question which only served to raise the ire of the doctor.

"What would you have of me?" he bristled angrily. "I heard they found nothing in his pockets so how can I say more. Science cannot give up the name of the dead, nor will it ever. The fact is he died of a wound to the abdomen. The rest is for others to determine, but not by asking of me the unanswerable."

At this outburst Doyle opened his mouth to speak, then thought the better of it. As undeserved as it was there could be no profit in provoking further argument. Yet there was still a look in his eyes which said he took such treatment hard.

The doctor noticed this and was about to round on him when the canon intervened softly.

"Do we know how long ago this happened?"

At that, doctor turned towards clergyman, his manner changing as he did so.

"Hard to say," he answered in a calmer, more professional, voice. "The cold preserved him remarkably well so he could have been there some time. How long only the people who put him there can say."

An answer which satisfied neither clergyman nor journalist although, if only for the sake of diplomacy, it was the canon who spoke.

"I understand. Perhaps if there are further developments you would be so kind as to let me know." His voice, quiet as it was, then took on a certain steel as he added, "And I would also consider it a great courtesy if you would do the same for my good friend Doyle."

At this the doctor could only stare. His deep breath clearly audible before he answered, "If you would have it that way then so be it."

His manner, his voice, even the expression on his face said it would be done only out of respect for the canon. But for that Doyle would be told nothing. Nevertheless, it had been agreed and it would be done which was a satisfactory arrangement for those concerned.

All that now remained was to discover why that still unknown man should have merited such a violent end. Who he was and why it so concerned the ravens also remained a mystery.

Chapter Eight

The Constabulary Take a Hand

Doyle was accustomed to the unpopularity his profession could sometimes bring. As he had long since discovered the making public of that which others would rather have kept secret would not make him liked, at least not by those whose secrets had just been revealed. In similar fashion those he had to sometimes question were not always happy to be asked. Dual reasons why his could be an unpopular face in an unpopular profession.

This he had come to accept as the hidden price of performing his role within that much larger society of which we are all a part. A vast collection of citizens who, it must be said, were often times well served by those who would enquire into areas some might want to keep hidden. Their praise, or even their thanks, for those who would do such a thing might always be muted, but it was a valuable service, nevertheless. A fact beyond dispute.

That being the case it is possible to imagine the surprise felt by Doyle on walking into a police station to be met not by sullen silence, but by a smile. Hardly a particularly welcoming smile it has to be admitted, but still a smile.

"There are people here hoping you would show up," Sergeant Fraser told him.

"Must be the company I keep," Doyle found himself saying, thinking perhaps the canon had used his influence.

An assumption which, as he discovered, was entirely wrong. The canon had done no such thing. The proof of it coming from the mouth of Sergeant Fraser.

"That I can't answer to, but they want to see you. Come through and I'll take you to them."

So saying he opened a door into what Doyle knew to be the inner sanctum. The place where only the police were usually allowed, journalists never. A strange state of affairs indeed thought Doyle as, curiosity piqued, he followed the sergeant down a short corridor to where he respectfully knocked on an unmarked door.

Inside, once permission to enter had been given, he saw two men waiting, one of whom was not in uniform. A detective as could easily be guessed. That latest addition to the constabulary whose duty was to investigate crimes once discovered and who were allowed to go without uniform, the better to associate with those who were the subject of such investigations.

Inspector Allaby, as he introduced himself, making it clear that of the two he was the one in charge. He was a stocky individual with wiry hair and far too much nervous energy. So much so he could barely stay still throughout the entire interview.

"And Inspector Marchant," the other, uniformed, man added. He was older and seemingly of a much more down to earth, pragmatic nature bordering on the curt. An attitude it seems to which all police officers are fated, eventually.

The introductions then being completed by a brief, if cordial, handshake, Inspector Allaby wasted no more time.

"We've heard about you," he told Doyle, giving no indication as to whether that information was to the good or otherwise. "And I ask no questions about how you came to find the body," he added in a voice, and with a look, that made it clear he believed the full story had not been told. "I concern myself only with the fact that it was you. You see, whoever killed our victim took great pains to hide him for which he must have had a good reason. Because of that we fear what will happen should the discovery of the body be revealed in *The Chronicle* or elsewhere."

"We wish the murderer to be kept uninformed while we conduct our investigation," Inspector Marchant said. "That will give us a freer hand."

"When we're not busy patrolling the bridge," Sergeant Fraser added with a baleful look at Doyle.

There being no malice in the comment Doyle merely acknowledged it with a slight nod and even slighter smile before replying to the two police inspectors.

"Your position is appreciated," he began slowly. "But this is a story which should be told, at some point."

In reply, Inspector Allaby laughed softly as if to say he understood completely, which he most likely did. A man of his rank and profession could no doubt be expected to have dealt with journalists on many occasions in the past, and likely to do so again in the future.

"Then I offer you a bargain," he said, foregoing what he already knew would be tedious, and futile, negotiations. "If *The Chronicle* stays silent on this until the murderer is caught you may have the full story. Is that acceptable to you?"

"But how will I know the full story?" Doyle asked in return. He too had experience of his own in such situations.

A fact obviously understood by the inspector who simply nodded, a slight smile about his lips.

"We will undertake to keep you informed. You will also be invited to witness anything as may be pertinent. That should be satisfactory reward I feel, but be certain," here he looked hard at Doyle, "in return your complete silence is expected."

To this Doyle nodded. The arrangement was fair and allowed the forces of the law free rein to catch a murderer for which he could make no complaint. The more so as he had his own reasons for seeking answers to this crime.

"You have my word," he answered.

The bargain being sealed by those words, and the obligatory handshake, the police were therefore able to pursue their investigation. How it would progress was something Doyle could only wait to find out although he did have one final thought on the subject. For reasons of good manners and good relations it was mentioned to no-one yet he knew that within the bargain just made with him was the tacit admission that the police still didn't know any facts about the dead man.

That being the case this was a mystery that would not soon be unravelled. Yet for all that, what was he to do. His word kept him gagged, metaphorically at least, so much as it went against his nature he could only wait until called for. After that he would see what he would see. Until then he could only be patient and hope others would do their duty, and keep to their bargain for which, even though he chafed at the delay, he could only wait for something to happen.

As might be guessed, being contacted by the police was the event that Doyle had been waiting for. To be contacted by Doctor Stanhope was an event he could hope for, but with very little expectation. The doctor, he felt, might just take it upon himself to tell only the canon of any fresh developments, leaving it to him to inform the man he was now calling his good friend Doyle. That may have been to slander the doctor who had, it should be remembered, given his word and yet despite that Doyle still had his reservations. Should he be contacted with further information it would most likely be by the police, of that he was certain.

How then to explain his thoughts when, in place of the runner he was expecting, a young cleric arrived, out of breath and embarrassed. His mission, it seemed, being to fetch Doyle not at the request of the canon, but for his comfort. To aid in a malady that was afflicting him. A mystery indeed and yet one which could be resolved easily, Doyle was sure, as he struggled into his coat to follow the cleric. Along the way he had hoped to glean further information, but that was not to be. The cleric knew very little.

As best as could be ascertained a messenger had arrived from Doctor Stanhope for which reason some unnamed member of staff went in search of the canon. What happened after that the young cleric had no idea other than the messenger was dismissed and it was decided that he, Doyle, should be sent for. More than that the innocent cleric had not been told although, to the slight discomfiture of Doyle, he did add that the messenger had instructions to call on him next. Doctor Stanhope it seemed had kept true to his word.

So, beyond knowing that he was invited to attend on the doctor in the mortuary Doyle had no guess as to why he might be needed elsewhere. Not, that is, until he was ushered into the rooms belonging to the canon. Then he had no reason to ask further. The brandy glass and decanter told their own story.

On the table next to the clergyman they stood, mute witness the cause of his malady and why it had been kept hidden from the messenger. For reasons so far unexplained the man was in his cups. Face flushed, eyes glazed, he was obviously seeking solace, but from what? What was it that had made the man so melancholic he had taken to the brandy?

Doyle was prepared to take a guess.

"So soon you give up the fight?" he asked softly.

On hearing his voice the canon stirred to look at him through unfocussed eyes.

"Care to join me?" he asked, reaching unsteadily for the brandy, and then as Doyle stayed still, he added miserably, "No. Suppose not. Why would you need it when you can still face your God."

"As can you if you would ask Him," Doyle replied, but said no more.

This was a crisis long in the making. Doyle knew that. He had seen it taking hold of the canon, eating into him until it could be fought no longer. Had he been more alert to the feelings of the other he might have expected it. Perhaps he should have expected it when no-one else could since no-one else but he knew the cause.

Its cause yes, but not its manifestation. He still had no idea in what way the canon had been affected, or when it would be shown. All he could do was wait and hear the man out until he felt able to reveal his innermost thoughts. Then a way might be found to resolve what was clearly a crisis of conscience.

In some eyes it might even have been a crisis of faith, but that Doyle doubted. The clergyman still had God, he was just unable to face Him. To the suggestion from Doyle that he talk to God the canon could only give a tragic look.

"And when I'm asked about such violence as we've seen how should I answer?" he asked mournfully. All of them. Those I let be taken by my weakness."

At last, it was revealed. It was those unfortunates who had met their end on the bridge that was the source of his misery.

"You showed them compassion when no-one else would," Doyle reminded him. "God could not call that a weakness."

"Yet the result was the same," the canon would not be moved. "They were taken while I did nothing to prevent it. How can I answer that charge?"

"With honesty. Your intentions were good. Who could ask more than that?"

Intending to calm the man, to offer him reassurance, instead it seemed Doyle had set off the explosive charge, if it could be so described.

"Good intentions," the canon almost sobbed. "Only one road is paved with good intentions and we both know where it leads."

By the look of him some would say he was there already. For sure he was suffering its torments.

"Not because of anything you did," Doyle was able to tell him, on surer ground now the root of the crisis had been revealed. "You may not have saved their bodies, but what of their souls? Those taken at the bridge were considered suicides by all, even me. You it was who held out. But for you they would have lain unsanctified."

At his words the canon gave a gasp of comprehension. His face changing as he considered them further.

"You mean...?" he asked, not daring to believe his own thoughts.

"I mean against the devilry on the bridge stood the compassion of Canon Jefferies," Doyle answered softly, yet with conviction. "For that, many souls are in your debt."

A brief silence followed his words during which all manner of emotions vied with each other on the face of the canon. Sometimes fear, sometimes doubt, sometimes revelation, understanding, hesitation or humility. Finally tranquillity appeared. The canon now at peace with himself.

"Is it true?" he asked, still not daring to believe.

In answer Doyle merely nodded. The smile on his face saying more.

Enough in fact to satisfy the canon who sat back in his chair, no longer in need of brandy. His crisis over he could face God again without fear of the afterlife. Better still he could face the mortal world again. At least, he could once the liquor wore off. Until then he needed to sit quietly, perhaps to sleep, which is where Doyle left him.

He had another invitation to keep and so he needed to go and yet, as he regained the street, he saw a single raven looking down on him from its tree top perch.

"The doubting is over," he told that black sentinel without thinking it strange.

His answer was a long, low, call which may have been approval, may have been thanks, or it may have been something else entirely. When ravens were involved no mortal man could know their real purpose. At least, not in any detail. That they were in this world to be in some ways servants, in some ways guardians, of Man could be accepted. It was how they chose to do it that would be forever unknown. Reason enough for Doyle to give it no further thought while on his way to the mortuary and his appointment with Doctor Stanhope.

It was while on his way there that Doyle finally understood the canon. As might be expected just then he could think of naught else until, at last, he was able to come to a conclusion. At which he knew, or believed he knew, why the canon had reached his crisis when he did. The timing of it became clear, as did the blame.

Perhaps blame was too strong a word and yet in ways Doyle was only just starting to comprehend he knew he was in some part accountable. That had to be so because it was his intervention that had brought matters to such a head. In his defence he had acted with the best of intentions which at any other time would have been justification enough although now that would never be sufficient. Not when he could still remember what the canon had said about the road paved with good intentions and where it led. It seemed he too needed to search his soul.

Doing that, however, still brought him back to the canon. If Doyle was right, and he believed he was, the knowledge that darker forces were involved when those on the bridge met their end had brought with it the first stirrings of guilt. Unjustified it may have been, but the canon always would be of the type that accepted the troubles of the world as his own. That being so the guilt he had not done more to save them would have grown. In his eyes, and to his frame of mind, had he not been so eager to have those deaths ruled as accidental the investigation into them could have started sooner. The thought of it made his guilt grow all the more.

For a while he was able to keep it at bay by his nights on the bridge; not a vigil but a penance. His way of holding back his personal demons until, that is, Doyle stopped him. Done for the best of reasons it was true yet it left the canon idle and so vulnerable to those thoughts that had preyed on his soul. The thoughts that had eaten into him until the only answer was brandy.

All of this Doyle now understood. His own guilt at not seeing it sooner he would deal with later, which he was resolved to do. For the moment, however, there was the more pressing matter of whatever awaited him at the mortuary and those who were there already. In this it seemed he was the last to arrive.

"By yourself?" Doctor Stanhope asked, no doubt expecting the canon to be with him.

"His Grace sends his apologies," Doyle replied shamelessly. "Affairs of church keep him occupied."

To this the reaction of the doctor was perhaps best described as a snort before he moved away to leave Doyle in the company of Inspector Allaby who was also there together with officers.

"We heard you were invited," the inspector told him, presumably to explain why no message had been sent by them.

"As I was," Doyle answered, "but without being told why."

His look as much as his words carried the question to which the inspector had a ready answer.

"The body has been claimed," he said briskly, to the point. "We now wait to see who will collect it so we may discuss the matter with him."

"And be told a name," Doyle added, seeing where this might head until a question entered his mind. "How was it known there was a body here to be claimed?"

"That we also expect to be told," the inspector replied, giving Doyle a look so searching as to be almost an accusation.

"Not from me," the accused man told him in tones of affronted dignity as was only to be expected.

"So we believe," came the police reply. "We did wonder, but then we were told your word could be relied on."

"My thanks to that man," Doyle answered in a manner which may be imagined, but which was perfectly natural for one whose word was doubted. An attitude which caused the inspector to smile slightly as he nodded in the direction of Doctor Stanhope.

"Him?" Doyle was incredulous.

The inspector smiled again. "Make no mistake, if he had his way you'd be packed off to report on the colonies, but he was honest enough to confirm your word could be trusted."

There was no exaggeration in saying Doyle was

dumbfounded. Indeed, of all those he might have expected to vouch for him Doctor Stanhope was far from prominent on that list. Apparently the man had put his honour before his antagonism which spoke highly of the doctor while also putting Doyle in something of a quandary. Simply put he had no idea what to do next.

There was no doubt he owed the doctor some measure of gratitude. At the very least an acknowledgement of the service he had just performed. Equally, however, there was just as little doubt the doctor would reject all signs of thanks, from him especially. So, what was he to do. Could he let the matter rest unresolved without that being considered the basest of ingratitude.

A difficulty for sure yet, after admittedly a very brief period of thought, there was no other way Doyle could find. His only course of action, it seemed, was to feign ignorance of everything the doctor had done on his behalf and conduct any further conversation in that same vein. Without being told he was sure the doctor would prefer it that way even if it did leave the debt unpaid. As to that Doyle could only hope for the chance to even the account at some later date.

Until then he would act as if Inspector Allaby had said nothing and simply follow whatever instructions the police chose to give. For him that meant taking station next to Sergeant Fraser who, of them all, was apparently pleased the canon had been unable to attend. The deeds as might happen that night not being suitable for the likes of him, so the sergeant said. That there might be deeds not suitable for a man of the cloth to witness was something else on which he held a firm opinion.

"There's more to this than you know," he muttered quietly to Doyle by way of changing the conversation.

"You've been told?" Doyle asked in return to which the sergeant shook his head.

"Don't need to be," he answered. "When villains fall out it's a club to the back of the head or a razor to the throat. They don't often hide it either. There's more to this than is being said or else why are they here."

By this he made it clear he was referring to the inspectors Marchant and Allaby.

"They don't turn out for just anything," the sergeant finished, this time with a knowing nod of the head.

What they did turn out for he failed to mention which in its own way was an admission he knew no more. Understandable perhaps as those of lower rank are seldom privy to the thoughts of their superiors. True in the police or any other organisation with a hierarchy to maintain. For which reason he could expect to hear no more and wait for orders to be given. A situation in which Doyle was his equal.

The two of them now sank back further into the shadows at the given command. Like everyone else bar the doctor and Inspector Allaby it was time to be hidden. The two men remained in the light to greet whoever it was coming to claim the body. This, if Doyle understood correctly, was to help restrain the person they were expecting and also to ensure the doctor was protected should events go the way Sergeant Fraser feared.

117

As to that time alone would tell. Until then they could only wait in the dark, saying nothing lest they be overheard. For the police a position with which they were all too familiar, but for Doyle it was a trial. Having neither training nor experience in such things he took it hard and found both his thoughts and his gaze wondering.

Unbidden, his eyes turned firstly towards the light where the two men were conversing in low tones beside the table on which lay the body found in the marsh. Now no more than a sheet-covered corpse which even in that place of the dead still created a faintly macabre air. Its very presence, remember, being for the sole purpose of attracting others unknown. A task for which only its maker could have foreseen.

Away from that scene there was nothing to attract the eye or the thoughts. Nothing except deep shadow until, that is, a faint tapping could be heard. Over as soon as it started yet it was enough to attract the attention; surely its purpose. Somewhere in that stygian darkness a creature wanted its presence to be known.

The unmistakeable form of a raven had come to witness the events, and it was not alone. As Doyle looked another raven appeared at a different window, followed by a third. Three ravens standing silently; waiting, as were their human counterparts, for whatever would happen next.

That it would happen soon was now guaranteed as the ravens were not prone to waiting long. They, of all creatures, would know how to judge their arrival.

From the shadows footsteps could be heard: slow, yet purposeful. Unseen at first yet unmistakable; someone was coming, bringing answers, or so it was hoped. The footsteps coming ever closer.

Stepping into the light there now came a sturdy individual. By dress and bearing a labourer yet with a physical appearance that denied he did much in the way of honest toil. A thief, then. One of the criminal underclasses whose hand would be turned to anything dishonest which was why he lacked the finely honed muscles of his law-abiding brethren.

"I've come for what's mine," he announced, his eyes on the shrouded body.

"And you can be sure it's yours?" Doctor Stanhope asked as he pulled back the sheet to reveal the ghastly face beneath.

Where an honest man might have flinched at the sight this individual merely nodded almost in satisfaction.

"A name, man. Give him a name," Inspector Allaby told him perhaps more brusquely than he intended. Now was not the time to be raising suspicions.

Not that any were raised in this man who seemed intent only on claiming the body as his and leaving soon after. His motives still unclear, but his greed all too obvious.

"That's Joe. Joe Malloy," he answered. "Known him for years."

"Indeed," Doctor Stanhope murmured. "So, is it you medical science needs to treat with when we come to his disposal?"

At that the unknown stranger gave a sly smile. Ignoring Inspector Allaby, whom he still took to be another doctor, he said, "There's one I know of who would like it. But if you have an offer to make..."

Head cocked to one side he waited for the bargaining to begin. Had he noticed the frown spreading over the face of the inspector, both at the interruption by Doctor Stanhope and at the reply, he might have thought differently. He might even have been suspicious, but by then greed had him in its grip. Blinded by it he failed even to take note of the sign the inspector made or the way the man moved to stand between him and Doctor Stanhope.

His first sense of any pressing danger came when the inspector spoke.

"We must talk about that, but not here."

At those last words the stranger gave a startled look. Eyes darting about he finally saw uniformed police approaching. At that, realising he was in a trap about to be sprung, he twisted, turned, tried to run. All to no avail. The police all around him, restraining him despite his cries and oaths unfit for printing.

Yet there was still more to tell. More indeed. Coming from the window a single loud cry of the ravens. Coming from the darkness the sound of running feet. The stranger had not been alone. Others had come with him, but stayed behind in the darkness, Now, hearing the sounds of his capture, they were intent only on escape.

With a muffled oath and order combined Inspector Marchant lead the chase. His men around him, they ran through the room, into the darkness, only to return minutes later with a disgusted shake of the head. The others, the accomplices, had made good their escape.

"Come to help you carry it did they?" Inspector Allaby looked at the prisoner they still had who returned his look with an insolent expression. Facts which confirmed this was by no means the first time he had been in the hands of the police.

No doubt the same could be said of his accomplices as Doyle realised with a slow comprehension. Had they come into the mortuary proper, come right up to the body, there would have been a scene not fit for the canon to witness. To that extent, then, Sergeant Fraser had been right in his prediction which Doyle acknowledged with a slight smile. The nod of understanding which passed between them being enough to complete their unspoken communication.

The inspectors, meanwhile, were gathered round the prisoner who had yet to give his name. In fact he had yet to say anything leaving his motives for being there still unfathomable.

"Come for the body did you?" Inspector Marchant said, stating what was surely obvious no doubt in the hope of provoking an answer.

When none immediately came Doctor Stanhope snorted. "As I suspected you intended to sell it. There's a few shillings worth lying there and you wanted it for yourself. Fresh corpses are all well and good for those who want to teach anatomical medicine and you can believe me when I say even these days there will be more who want to teach than there are bodies to do it with." He stopped there to give the prisoner a look of the kind Doyle had thought was reserved exclusively for him. "But that's not what this one was after," he continued. "There's others who want to study how the human organs decay over time. The better to determine when a body died should you police want to know. That's where this one was headed. Such a perfectly preserved specimen would be highly prized by those

121

bent on studying the pathology of it."

Here both inspectors gave understanding nods to show that in their view that particular mystery at least was solved. Any other questions, as they knew, would best be answered when the prisoner was safe in custody. An operation which began with the prisoner being led away until, that is, Inspector Allaby held up a restraining hand.

"Answer me this," he said, turning to the doctor. "For the effects of a death to be studied, or the decay it causes, would the examiner have to be told when it happened?"

"No use otherwise," The doctor answered. "How else could the rate of decay be measured?"

"As I thought. So this one here must know far more about the murder than he cares to admit."

With a chuckle completely devoid of all humour he turned back to the prisoner now finally starting to look worried, more than worried. The fear in his eyes obvious to all. Even more so when the inspector spoke again, his voice now grim.

"Take him away. Looks like he's got an appointment with the gallows."

Chapter Nine

A Labyrinth of Villains

Once again inside the confines of the police station Doyle was faced with a mixture of anticipation and frustration. Anticipation because he was waiting for the police to finish their interview with the still unnamed prisoner and frustration because he was not allowed to be a part of it. Against regulations, so he was told. How much of that was true, he could only guess, though he had a suspicion it was close to the mark.

His companion as he waited was Sergeant Fraser who was far from pleased at the outcome.

"Should've had them all," he muttered, that being his opinion.

His opinion of the inspectors he kept to himself yet, despite that, he did go as far as predicting their likely behaviour.

"They'll turn it to the good," he announced with certainty. "You watch. You don't get to be like them without being able to turn it to the good."

Exactly what he meant by that Doyle had no way of knowing, nor could he ask. Before the question had even been framed the inspectors were back; neither of them looked happy.

"He hardly said a word," Inspector Allaby told Doyle before he could ask. "Too frightened to say anything."

At which he shook his head, perhaps at the thought of it or perhaps as he remembered the fruitless interview, who could say. It could even have been both. The tribulations of those who would upkeep the law were often manifold.

That the interview had been fruitless was beyond question. During the interview, the prisoner had revealed his name to be Elijah Jackson, but had given up very little else. Most likely because the journey to the police station had given him the chance to compose himself. If not then the rogue had just decided to brazen it out. Not that the reason mattered. As far as the police were concerned all that counted was his reticence and in that he was absolute.

"Admit you intended to sell the body," Inspector Allaby had challenged him.

In reply he shrugged insolently. "Can't blame a man for trying to make an honest profit."

"But first you had to know it was there," Inspector Marchant then joined in the assault at which the freshly named Elijah Jackson continued in his insolence.

"I heard tales."

Plainly this could have no end. With the man confirmed in his attitude they could expect no answers of any consequence. A fact confirmed in some way when Inspector Marchant pursued his theme further.

"You must have done more than heard talk. As the doctor

said unless you could estimate the date of his demise the body would be worthless. So how could you know that?"

The prisoner shrugged then gave a petulant grin, saying nothing. It seemed he intended to simply lie to whichever pathologist would buy the corpse from him. His word was as false as his claim to body. Did he have any conscience at all?

For sure there was none the inspectors could find as they stared at him in disgust. A look he returned with no hint of shame. Still the air of insolence was about him as Inspector Allaby now leant forward, his face serious.

"So now we have you as a self-confessed fraudster you can tell us what really happened. Who killed the man you identified as Joseph Malloy?"

The question, asked forcefully, finally provoked a response. Elijah's eyes betrayed a flicker of fear. No more than that and soon gone, but it was enough.

"You can't expect me to tell you that," he answered, softly this time.

"You'd rather face gaol?"

"I'll take my chances," he told them, his meaning clear. It was not the thought of imprisonment which scared him. It was falling foul of whoever had committed the murderous deed that was his fear.

"So what do you propose?" Doyle asked after the interview had been relayed to him in full. Surely the police would not abandon such a promising (in fact, their only) source of information.

There, it seemed, he need have no worries. Plans were already afoot to bring about a change to the rogue currently in their custody.

"We've decided to let him go," the inspector said and then, at the surprised look from Doyle, he explained further. "He knows too much for the murderer, our real quarry, to be happy, especially once it's heard he's been talking to us." There he nodded his head knowledgeably before he continued with what could only be described as savage satisfaction. "Once he realises others are after him, and what will happen should they catch him, it's a good wager he'll want to make a trade in return for our protection."

"And you intend to start now?" Doyle looked at him to see the other shake his head confidently.

"Not yet," he answered with the same satisfaction as before. "Let him wait a while and review his situation. Give it time to let the word spread too. Those not caught before will soon be telling their own tale. We can rely on them for that."

"Turning it to the good," Doyle stated to see a brief smile, soon hidden, on the face of Sergeant Fraser.

To their good fortune Inspector Allaby had his back to the sergeant and so failed to see any levity in the comment.

Taking it at its face value he simply nodded in agreement. "Just so. How policing is really done."

Faced with such an assertion Doyle could only nod, about to ask when all of this would start until the inspector gave him a strange look.

"Tell me this," he began, "these doctors who buy dead bodies, filthy trade as it is, would you know who they are?"

Taken by surprise at this Doyle could only shake his head. Much as he knew people who could supply him with information none of them were in the medical profession, besides which who would admit to such dealings. On this subject, then, he had no idea who they were or where they could be found.

"Nor do I," the inspector told him, speaking slowly. "So if neither the press not the police know who these people are, how does Mr Elijah Jackson have their acquaintance?"

A mystery indeed and one which could be answered that same evening, assuming events proceeded in the way the inspector hoped, that is. For himself Doyle had to admit to having doubts. Such plans rarely went smoothly. Even so in his own mind he was sure of one thing: the ravens were not needed tonight. No doubt they would be there, but on this night Man alone should be sufficient, or so he thought. Time alone would prove him wrong.

First, however, there was an expedition to a certain part of the city to consider. That part which was both the reason why the city had come about and the cause of it having such a black name. As with all cities the two were intertwined and always for the same reason. An event usually described as progress, by all those who lived elsewhere.

To explain, the one unmistakeable way in which our modern lives differ from those of our forebears is due in its entirety to machines. Because of them the craftsmen of old has all but vanished with all our goods, household and military, now being machine made; factory made. Increasingly we favour the product of machines collected together in factories for their greater efficiency over the work of a single artisan.

As a consequence of this ever more people, whose ancestors

would have toiled the fields, are now finding employment in those same factories. That being the change previously mentioned. No longer do people work in the fields and live in hamlets around them. Now they work in factories and live in the cities which grew around them to service their needs.

Inevitable perhaps and it has to be admitted we all of us derive much comfort from those things which are now manufactured. In many ways we have even come to depend on these things. So much so that we have allowed ourselves to become blind to the, also inevitable, consequences of what has indeed been a rapid change.

By this is meant the way in which the city itself came to grow. How that vast collection of streets and houses, which is a city defined, came to be. Then perhaps some sense might be made of it all and the city as it is presently constituted better understood. Its citizens, of course, would take more understanding, possibly combined with the tolerance of a Canon Jefferies, but the city and all its byways would at least be more sensible. As would the next part of this tale.

Before then, however, it needs to be remembered that as the factories, mills and engineering works continued to open so ever more people were needed to fill them. For which reason houses had to be built, followed by yet more as the demands of the factories increased. None of which was done in any kind of planned manner. Houses were needed so houses were built by whoever owned, or bought, any piece of land available.

The result of this was soon plain to see. These houses were small and packed together to the profit of those who wanted the greatest number in the smallest space. The same reason why the streets between them were so narrow. Also because of this streets were short and not always connected to each other. Many would end where the walls of other houses began in a dead end. As for those that did lead somewhere they would be crossed by other streets, placed by other builders whose only concern was their own interests.

In summary then the section of the city where lived those who worked in the factories and the mills was cramped, dark and crowded. Its streets followed no pattern, making it nonsensical to try and describe them as a maze. There was, in short, no order and no plan; just a jumble of buildings put together by no guiding hand in which the angels themselves could be lost forever.

This was where Doyle now found himself. In darkened streets where lights were few and shadows long. Where he was an outsider almost. There to report on events as they happened in what could by some standards be regarded as a foreign country that was also part of the same city he lived in. This was not a world the press ever visited. Even those who wrote stories lamenting on the unhappy lot of the poor usually did so at a safe distance, knowing better than to visit a place where the police walked in pairs for their own self-protection.

A bad area, then, where the people made the place and the place made the people. One of them being the previously mentioned Elijah Jackson who was now abroad on those same streets. After being released from police custody he was back in his own world if it would have him. In which lay the rub.

If Inspector Allaby was right in his assessment the rogue had witnessed the murder, possibly even helped to hide the body. For sure he knew all about it. Too much in fact. That was why he had no need to guess why the police could be seen at the marshes, or what they had taken away. He knew and, for reasons so far unexplained, he knew how much a dead body was worth.

That, of course, was his undoing. Knowing its value he became blinded by greed. Uncaring of any risk he elected to have it for himself and in so doing he was caught. The result being other members of his gang, and it had to be assumed there was a gang, would now have been told, courtesy of those he took with him to the mortuary. If so the question was – what would the gang make of such a state of affairs?

According to Inspector Allaby, who was sure of it, then the aforesaid Elijah Jackson had no choice in the matter. His only chance now was to try and make his peace with this murderous gang in the certain knowledge that if he failed his life was surely forfeit. A chance for which Inspector Allaby was prepared to give very little.

"He knows too much," he announced shortly before releasing the man. "Why should they take the risk?"

A grim assessment to be sure, but most likely accurate. Once the police knew he could lead them to those implicated in the murder, as they now did, the life of Elijah Jackson was at grave risk from those self-same people.

"Worth more to them dead," Sergeant Fraser muttered in ghoulish humour.

Reason enough for the rogue to trade such information as he possessed for the protection only the police could offer. Once, that is, he came to realise it was his only option.

Something which was expected to happen that same night. A fact, or an opinion, given to explain why the police were there in number; hoping to prevent the untimely death of Elijah Jackson and, perhaps, to catch those villains as would want to be the cause of it.

Here the presence of Doyle requires little in the way of explanation as the reader will doubtless have realised he was there with the police, as indeed he was. It need not be imagined, however, that he was there at their invitation. Quite the contrary, they would rather he stayed away. The actual business of police work being deemed too dangerous for such as he, or so he was told by more than one.

In all due fairness it has to be said the police were thinking only of his safety even if Doyle would have none of it. To his eyes he had been promised the opportunity to see the investigation through and that he intended to do. For the rest of it he would trust his luck, he answered. At this, perhaps naturally, there was a certain impasse until eventually the police relented; their heads shaking as they did so.

Dire warnings were given and it was made clear they could accept no responsibility should any harm befall him. It was also made clear the police had priorities before his safety so it would not do to expect their help, or even to look for it. He would be, in their words, on his own.

Only when Doyle accepted this, and said so, was he allowed to join them as they spread themselves out in that part of the city where few dared to go. Brief facts to explain why he was, as previously described, on those dark and dimly lit streets. Around him, if for a while, the forces of the law as represented by Sergeant Fraser and an unnamed constable, both now looking at him with a mixture of respect and pity. Respect because he was man enough to accept the risks and pity because he was foolish enough to take them. Police sergeants and constables, it seemed, had their own way of looking at the world.

That notwithstanding, he was there and they were resigned to the fact.

"Probably better like this," Sergeant Fraser muttered with a look that, this time, held more pity than respect. "Else ways you'd have just gone off on your own."

In answer to which Doyle borrowed the police habit of putting his head to one side while he thought about it before giving a shrug and as much of a grin as he dared without causing too much in the way of antagonism. Now was not the time to cause any upset. Rather it was a time to be careful as, together, they walked the short length of the street to the corner. Around that who knew what dangers lurked.

As Doyle understood it the rogue Elijah Jackson would already be in what those of a literary disposition usually described as a den of thieves. A place where those of his kind would meet, drink copious amounts of ale and boast of their latest villainies. Most likely it was also the place where further outrages were planned.

Even so the question on which everything else hinged was whether Elijah Jackson would still be welcome there. The wager being he had transgressed against their own code for which there could only be one punishment. That night, perhaps on the streets outside, he would meet his end. The other wager being he would be quick-witted enough to avoid this which, as Doyle was to learn later, was exactly how it happened, with the help of the constabulary.

They saw him leaving the kind of establishment to which the law-abiding were best advised not to visit. They also saw him in the company of three others. As he walked, Elijah Jackson was constantly changing his position within that small group; trying not to be surrounded by them. The implication was obvious. This apparently friendly group were really his executioners and he knew it best of all.

This left the police in a dilemma. To intervene too early would be disastrous while too late would be fatal. Their actions, therefore, had to be timed to perfection even though they could only watch from a distance. Too far to offer any immediate help or to prevent the thrust of a knife yet unable to move any closer. Policing in the raw indeed.

Their anxiety rising they could only watch as the group in question made its way to a street corner, soon to be out of sight. A few steps, no more, and it would be done. The group beyond their view. Elijah Jackson beyond their help. His fate out of their hands.

Out of his own hands also, or so it appeared. At the corner itself they stood, no longer with any pretence at friendship. Pretence gone they put hands on him, pulling him into the street beyond. The rogue struggled against it, but to no avail. Their grip was firm as they dragged him into a street from which he would never return.

Clearly the time for action, the police charged. Two in number yet still they ran, their duty clear. They came to his aid and as they did so they called out. Calls for assistance and calls of their presence. Calls to let the gang know they were there and calls to stop their unlawful deeds.

At the sound of them they froze, Elijah Jackson tearing himself free as both parties clashed. Other calls now to be heard: answering calls. More police on their way. Too many for the ruffians now trying to flee.

Soon all was confusion. A mêlée in which the ruffians, at first outnumbering the police, fought to escape. The police, in turn, unable to stop them and unwilling to try. Their first task the safety of Elijah Jackson. Even so, as more police answered and the ruffians fled, it became evident even that was too much.

Taking advantage of the confusion, the rogue had run off. Yet as he ran the shouts of the police now giving chase were joined by other shouts. Calls from those who would do him harm. He was not just a marked man. He was a hunted man and those who held the advantage wanted only his death.

Unknowing of this Doyle and his police companions heard the shouts, knew what they signified, but as yet could do no more. The cries echoing along narrow streets and round many corners until even their direction was impossible to guess. Perforce, then, they could only wait until the sound of running feet could be heard. The chase was heading their way. Heading their way and soon on them. Without warning Elijah Jackson rounded the corner, wide-eyed and breathless. His pace alone forcing him past those waiting who would have turned to run after him except in that they were prevented. Almost before they could gather their wits, and their balance, two more ruffians appeared.

Plainly after Elijah Jackson as they were, and surprised by the police as they also were, the ruffians were at first taken aback. The police too, it should be said, were equally caught unawares so that, for a brief second, both sides stood frozen. Then, recovering first, the police made to tackle the ruffians who, now also recovered, fought back vigorously. The fight ugly yet even handed.

For his part Doyle looked to the fight, then to Elijah Jackson. Seeing the rogue still in flight, and about to turn a street corner, the choice was made. He alone had to give chase, to be a hound chasing the fox so the huntsmen could follow. Above all their quarry must never be allowed to escape for if he did too many questions would remain unanswered.

In that vein he ran. Behind him the sounds of the struggle and shouts of others on their way. Friends or foes who could tell and ignored just the same. His sole purpose the rogue ahead of him. The man was now turning the corner, soon to be out of sight.

Redoubling his efforts Doyle soon reached that same street corner; turning it to see only empty street. The rogue had turned another corner, but which one. With so many to choose from, how could he know. Had the rogue eluded them?

At that thought Doyle slowed to a walk, no longer with any clear aim. Without direction until, that is, he heard the sound he should have expected: the harsh croak of a raven.

Silently they had arrived. Flying high over the rooftops to look down on the streets below; nothing hidden from their gaze. Not Doyle, not the police and especially not the path taken by Elijah Jackson. That now being indicated by a single raven swooping low into a side street.

With a grin that was almost a laugh Doyle began running again. At the corner he looked back to where uniformed figures could be seen at the far end of the street. A single wave to call them on and he was gone, still on the heels of his fox, a quarry now even further away and likely to escape.

For sure that was the thought of Elijah Jackson who knew he was running for his life and his freedom. With no desire to be at the mercy of either the law or lawbreakers he ran on. Around one more corner and even the lone figure pursuing him would be gone, or such was his figuring. He would escape, get away.

And he would have done had it not been for the ravens. Guardians of Man as they may have been, but not of this man alone. They too had their reasons for seeing this man caught. Even if his punishment was none of their concern his part in this puzzle must needs be recorded, or so they considered. That being the case, they acted, swooping down as one.

Turning the corner he saw them, all of them. Flying low, blocking the street as they flew at him. Their calls loud and harsh. Their eyes blazing, merciless, at one who could so easily collude in the murder of his fellow man.

From a distance Doyle saw the man stagger back, cowering against the wall as the ravens appeared. Streaming out from the side street they flew over him, around him, calling out to him. Calls no human need obey yet insistent just the same. He heard and he understood, most certainly he understood..

Perhaps out of fear, terror, or a stronger will he roused himself, lurching down the street as Doyle closed in. Behind

Doyle was the police, also gaining ground. Surely this was the end. The chase over.

An opinion not shared by the ravens. Two of them were now flying low over Doyle, calling out to him. A warning he was sure, but of what. Where was the danger and what form would it take?

He was soon to find out. From a side street ahead of him two ruffians emerged. Their eyes at first only on Elijah Jackson who desperately turned into another street. His breathing hard, laboured. A man at the end of his tether; defenceless against the ruffians.

Had he been alone that surely would have been the end of him. No raven could have stopped the thrust of a knife or the slash of a razor. It was to his good fortune then that Elijah Jackson was not alone that night. Beside him, or at least not far behind, were the police. His protectors as they now were. Those who would tackle the ruffians; one to be captured, one to escape.

Doyle in the meantime slipped past the fracas to follow Elijah Jackson. Now an easy task as the rogue had stopped running. Indeed, could go no further. The street itself ending in a brick wall from which there could be no escape. As such he was trapped, exhausted and about to be caught.

Knowing it he stood there, summoning up the last dregs of his defiance, his resistance growing until that too was destroyed. Not by man but by raven call. Three of them flying above him, calling harshly one after another to wear the rogue down.

The end coming, he backed against a wall watching the lone figure of Doyle walking slowly towards him. A dark shape against the light. More shadow than man. That is, it was covered by an altogether more monstrous shadow. That of a raven.

Flying low through the light cast by streetlamp, its shadow filled the street. Spreading across road and walls, heading towards the rogue. Other ravens now fell silent. The apparition, for such it was, reached out. Engulfing the rogue who could only stand shaking in fear as together the ravens gave one last call, harsh and loud.

Then they were gone. The sky clear as Doyle walked forward, now joined by uniformed figures; law keepers marching towards the lawbreaker who made it clear they could expect no further trouble from him.

He was defeated as he would soon prove by answering all their questions. Mysteries were about to be resolved.

CHAPTER TEN

REVELATIONS OF A VILLAIN

A question always difficult to answer is how much praise a man should accept. Should he, as some would have it, accept all that others had to give for to refuse it would be churlish. As an alternative should he refuse to accept any in the belief that the very essence of a man lies in his modesty. Who could say. Perhaps, as is so often the case, the answer occupies a more central position. A man should accept some praise, but only as much as his conscience allows. Anything more would be immodest.

Of course, all of this pre-supposes the praise to be fairly earned. That a man had indeed done all that he was being praised for. If not then what did it say about a man who would accept any of it. Could he do that and still consider himself to be a man as the term is generally understood.

Exactly the dilemma that now faced Doyle. On their return to the police station he had been praised by all. Even by Sergeant Fraser who he had thought would have been unhappy at the way he had deserted him and the constable during their fight with two of the miscreants.

"Not your place to get involved in any of that," the sergeant told him when he tried to make amends. "You did right by going after that blackguard Jackson and there's no-one can say any other."

As the reader may surmise the sergeant used a far more colourful epithet to describe the rogue, here omitted for the sake of decency.

In the setting of a police station, however, and the company being all male such language was not out of place, nor was comment made about it. Any words as were spoken were aimed mainly at Doyle and concerned his success at trapping the rogue. For this he was given great praise even by the two inspectors who without knowing it had just created the previously mentioned dilemma he was struggling to resolve. How to deny the unjustified praise while not being able to explain the true circumstances? At least, not without the police questioning his very sanity.

While it was true he could have mentioned the ravens and their part in the proceedings, who in the present company would have believed him? Most likely they would have considered it a feeble attempt at humour at best, or, just as likely, wondered about his sobriety. For sure they would never have believed it to be the literal truth it actually was. Reason enough to justify his silence rather than lose the good opinion in which he was currently held.

In his defence it should also be said his conscience forbade him from allowing the praise to become too fulsome. That would never do. So, for reasons that were mistaken for modesty, he quickly turned the conversation back to their captures and the story they had to tell.

Here, perhaps, a word of explanation is called for. As mentioned above the police had captives, all taken prisoner that evening. Three in all. The first being Elijah Jackson as needs no saying. The other two, as might also be guessed, were from those villains as had tried to hunt him down. One captured by Sergeant Fraser himself and the other by those who had followed Doyle as mentioned earlier in this tale.

Now with all those in custody, as it can be so described, there was every hope they would reveal all. Doyle certainly had hopes even though he knew this would still only answer the mystery of the dead man, Joseph Malloy. How that in turn would relate to the greater puzzle posed by the ravens he could only wait and see. Until then, of course, he had no choice but to wait for the answers which he had every right to expect would soon be forthcoming.

"Have they said anything?" he asked of no-one in particular. He was met with chuckles around the room.

"Had no choice," Inspector Marchant told him with great satisfaction. "They knew Elijah Jackson would soon be talking to us so if they said nothing it would go harder for them in court."

"And a pretty tale they told too," Inspector Allaby added with equal satisfaction.

It was at this point that Doyle regretted not being present when these villains were separately interviewed. Much as he wanted to be there, and much as he asked, it was always denied him. Against regulations, as he was once again told.

Most likely that was true although, from a different

perspective, it also signified the limits of the co-operation he had been promised. Apparently neither his silence nor the praise heaped on him, however unjustified, was sufficient for them to disregard those regulations as they referred to, but never described. In such manner does the official mind work.

The result of this being, somewhat naturally, that Doyle heard no story first hand. He had to be content with the narrative as told to him by the police Inspectors. While in many ways more convenient as he was spared the repetition of hearing the same story from more than one mouth it did nevertheless have its drawbacks. Of these the most frustrating to Doyle was that he heard only what the inspectors deemed relevant. Anything that might have had a bearing on that greater mystery would not be told him. Indeed, no-one would even know it for what it was. A problem, then, but one for which there was no solution. Doyle could only take the story as it was told. A story that came mainly from the mouth of Elijah Jackson. The other two miscreants provided confirmation and the occasional extra detail, but on the whole the story was his.

Its origin was that fateful night when police and excisemen had gathered at the dockside, their intention to capture smugglers. As previously described, while the police awaited their intended targets, clear sounds of another smuggler gang could be heard – this, it seemed, was Joseph's Malloy's gang, of which Elijah Jackson was a member.

On that night their task was to move illegally held items from a quayside warehouse to another location where they could be kept hidden, the exact nature of those illegal items not being something on which any of the parties involved would dwell. Contraband of some form, it was assumed, though no further questions were asked. All that mattered was how this story ended, not how it began.

On that night the devil was most certainly abroad, confounding the plans of men.

It was that night, as the reader will recall, which began with contraband being stowed on a boat to be transported up the river, work which had to be done quietly; stealthily, the all of them tense and alert for even the slightest of sounds. Through the mist that hid them from view as surely as it hid others from them, they heard the shouts of the police, of the excisemen, which to them could mean only one thing: they were caught.

They panicked. Their thoughts only of escape, they scattered; some taking to their heels, others thinking the boat was a safer refuge. Those who ran either escaping completely or finding themselves heading towards the otherwise occupied police, whereupon they turned and ran the other way. Their confusion complete.

As for those few on the boat their intention at first was to sail the boat further upriver until a place of safety was found, somewhere else on that river where they could jump ashore ahead of what they were sure would be a police pursuit. A plan that had considerable merit and had every chance of success, given the thick fog which helpfully obscured them all from view. Instead, Joseph Malloy took what was to be a fatal decision. The result of which would later cost him his life.

Realising the contents of that boat would incriminate them all he thus decided to be rid of it. To send it to a place where not even the police would be able to recover it. That place being, of course, the bottom of the river, where dark water would hide the evidence of their crimes.

Accordingly, then, this is what he set out to do.

"Tried to stop him, or so he said," Inspector Marchant added, speaking of Elijah Jackson. "But couldn't for fear of making too much noise."

An argument followed that was unassailable. Believing the police to be on their heels, the rogues were badly placed to argue. To their minds too much noise would further attract the very constabulary they were trying to avoid, for which there was but one solution. They had to remain silent; restricting their arguments to a few simple hand gestures and, perhaps, a look or two of disapproval. None of which had the slightest effect on Joseph Malloy.

So, as they gave up the fight and leapt ashore, he set the boat adrift and taking in water before joining them. The result of which being they were safe, but the contraband was lost.

"And that was his undoing," Inspector Allaby took up the tale as a means of moving it to an entirely different time and an entirely different location. In this case a day later when the gang assembled at a so far unnamed place to explain themselves to an also unnamed boss; the man in charge of their criminal enterprises who was now calling them to account for the loss of such a valuable cargo, whatever it may have been.

Here, the blame fell squarely on Joseph Malloy. By then, of course, the truth of the matter had been discovered, the police having no reason to keep their arrests secret. As a result of which it was plain their contraband was never in danger; in fact could have been sailed up the river without hindrance.

Its loss, therefore, being caused in its entirety by the panicked actions of that same Joseph Malloy, or so the others were then claiming.

In part, it should be said, this was due to the natural desire amongst those of low nobility to accept no blame if it could be deflected elsewhere although in the main this was more due to fear.

"A dangerous sort by their account," Inspector Marchant then added. "Could be all friendly one minute, slit your throat the next."

An assessment which was indeed accurate. As the tale was taken up again the remainder of the story soon unfolded; a story that was now not of contraband, but of murder; cold blooded murder.

Its protagonist, the still unnamed boss, now took centre stage, if such a theatrical term be permitted. A man who kept himself apart from others. A man who also delighted in carrying a sword on those occasions when he visited them, using it to point or to threaten entirely as he saw fit.

To him the sword was his symbol of authority, his mace. Once belonging to a knight, or so he claimed, that was certainly how it was used normally, as a means of gaining prestige over the ruffians he commanded.

Yet for all that it was still a weapon as he was about to prove. According to those there, once they explained themselves his face contorted with rage. Hard came his breathing, but from his lips not a sound. Accusation not made, discussion not necessary, he stood in front of the thoroughly terrified Joseph Malloy. Menace in his eyes, not his words.

All was silent. All was still. No-one dared to move, or utter a single word. As one they all waited. All attention on their leader who stood, eyes fixed on the man before him. The man who stood paralysed with fear.

With a single thrust of the sword it was done. The mortally wounded Joseph Malloy staggered back, then sank to the floor; life and blood both draining from him. His last sight the man standing over him, blood dripping from his sword, as a chilling smile almost of delight came to his face. Sentence passed and duly executed, he was their master, their lord, and no-one knew it better than he.

The proof of it lay on the ground beside him. A body whose soul had departed without a single raven call to mourn its passing. Now just the shell of what had once been, nothing and no-one, it seemed, would mourn the loss of what had gone. To those left alive the corpse was no more than an encumbrance, an inconvenience to be picked up and tossed away. Exactly what they did.

"Thrown in the river," Inspector Allaby completed the tale in a voice that rightly expressed his contempt for those who could do such a thing.

A sorry end to a life indeed, but hardly the end of the tale surely. There was still so much that remained unknown, in Doyle's eyes at least. Even if he accepted the tale just told there was nothing in it to explain why the ravens had involved him in all of this let alone why they had involved themselves. A conclusion he was fast reaching, indeed had reached by the end of the tale, it seemed other questions still remained to be answered.

Seeing his frown Inspector Allaby smiled a friendly smile.

"The place where it happened, the murder scene. We intend to visit it on the morrow. You'll be with us, I take it?"

Phrased as a question it may have been yet Doyle knew it to be the invitation it actually was, to which he readily accepted. Perhaps there, in that place where cold-hearted murder had taken place, he might find answers to the riddle set him by the ravens; some of them at any rate. That other question, the name of the man who had committed the foul deed, he expected to be answered that evening.

Alas that was not to be.

"Wouldn't tell us," Inspector Allaby said with a shake of the head. "Too scared of the man to even say his name."

By his tone he was as frustrated as Doyle, yet there was nothing to be done. If rogues such as those were too afraid of their chief to even reveal his name there was little the police could do to counter it. Not when all they had to offer was the threat of further imprisonment which, it could only be assumed, men such as they would take lightly. Certainly, it held less terror for them that than inspired by their leader.

Given that he was a man of obvious power and seemingly above their station in life, Doyle could only think of Jacob Arthan as fitting that particular bill. A thought made all the more concrete by the fact that the boat had been loaded from his warehouse, always assuming the ravens were correct. In this Doyle had every faith in them although in a different way that still left him with a problem. Namely, how to explain this to the police?

Reason enough for him to stay silent. Let the new day

bring forth its own revelations and let them be dealt with then. For now all he could do was place his faith in the efficiency of the police investigation.

Should anything more be required, of course, he knew he could always depend on the ravens. In ways only they could devise he would be guided, but to what end was still a mystery. As to that he could only hope it would happen soon, and that he was capable of understanding it when it happened. Something only time would tell.

CHAPTER ELEVEN

AT THE SCENE OF A MURDER

Having spent the better part of the day cajoling the canon out of his black mood, then being present at the mortuary as events there unfolded, Doyle had, by any reckoning, been fully occupied all day. Now, at the close of that same day, he longed for his bed and the sleep he would need in preparation for the following morning, which he was sure would be just as hectic and provide no respite nor rest.

It was, then, with some small annoyance, and a greater amount of surprise, that he found himself being accosted outside his lodgings by none other than Madame Clara.

What reason she had to seek him out and talk with him he did not know, but as he could hardly ignore her, and as inviting her into his lodgings was unthinkable, he could only wait for her to proceed, hiding his weariness out of common politeness. An act she either failed to notice or chose to ignore in her zeal to speak with him.

"There is a strangeness in the air," she announced, looking at him with accusing eyes. "A disturbance among the spirits which you are a party to and cannot deny."

Her words startled him, perplexed him even. A denial already on his lips, she cut him off with a stern shake of her head. Doyle was at a complete loss. What did she want of him, and why would she believe he had been dealing with the spirits? Such things were in her province entirely, as he was about to remind her, when she forestalled him with a look.

"You will remember when I attempted to contact the spirits in your presence. The night when we were interrupted by the ravens."

She stopped here as if waiting for him to take up the story. Clearly expecting him to provide some explanation when all he could do was nod his head to show he remembered the night, but he had nothing more to add.

"Come sir," Madame Clara now raised her voice. "I only saw them for an instant, you not even that., yet you knew what they were and alone of us all you were not the least bit alarmed. How could that be unless you knew why they were there?"

Doyle came to realise he was trapped. It was, of course, true that he knew the ravens were there. He also knew there was no reason to fear them, but how to explain that to Madame Clara? There indeed was the rub.

Had he been able to offer in an instant perhaps soothing words of little substance, they might have carried the day. Madame Clara might have been mollified, at least enough to let the matter rest. As it was, however, his silence was in itself an admission he knew far more than he was ready to disclose.

And yet a disclosure of some kind had to be made. Madame Clara would settle for nothing less. A disclosure or perhaps, he wondered, an exhortation. A way of preventing her from looking any deeper into the affair; something that would appeal to her own interest in the spirits, yet would prevent any further discussion on the subject.

To that end he looked at her, clear eyed, before saying, "There are dark forces currently adrift in this world. Forces which mean us great harm."

Before saying more he stopped, searching her face to see if she was taking this as seriously as it was intended.

Then, satisfied she was, he continued, "A higher authority has bade me stay silent so I can say no more, not until innocents are no longer at risk. After that, perhaps, we may talk again. But until then your silence is required, as is your discretion."

In all conscience he could say no more, nor did he intend to no matter how she might ask. For him this conversation was at an end which he signalled by turning towards the door of his lodgings.

On the threshold he stopped to look at her again.

"It would be best if you made no attempt to contact the spirits for a while," he told her, his voice soft yet holding authority.

At that he left, not sure if his last words had been sage advice or merely theatrics designed to ensure her silence. It was, however, kindly meant for he had no wish to see Madame Clara ensnared by the devilry he knew to be abroad. Too much of that had already happened and he doubted the ravens would come to her aid. Even less did he believe she would turn to the church for answers. She was not of that persuasion.

She was, instead, a woman who could hold her own counsel. By type, and by profession, she would accept that dark forces were loose, but how she would act on the news was something Doyle was unable to fathom. In that he was her equal as she too was, for the moment, undecided. For her more thought was needed, then her decision would be taken.

What would happen after that not even the ravens could foretell. In her future lay too many imponderables. Her decisions, and her actions, yet to be decided, her future could only be equally opaque. Her fate, therefore, would be of her own making even if none could say to what end that would be.

Certainly, Doyle could have no inkling. His thoughts being only of sleep he elected to do no more. Whatever happened next, he decided, could safely be left until after his slumber and that he proceeded to do. Being capable of no more he let sleep take him and found comfort in the arms of Morpheus.

As a result it was a much refreshed Doyle who faced the next morning. Refreshed, somewhat naturally, after a deep and undisturbed sleep although it should be said his mood was also pensive as he thought of the night before. More specifically he was thinking of the unexpected conversation with Madame Clara and what the result might be. Thoughts for which he could find no answer.

Good enough reason, then, to put such considerations from his mind and turn instead to the business of the day. That being more constructive, not to mention informative. This was, after all, the day on which the police were to visit that secret hideaway where the late Joseph Malloy met his untimely end.

While they didn't know the exact location, they could make an educated guess. As the still undisclosed cargo of contraband was to be transported by boat then their destination must have a dock. That being the case, and by no means a difficult deduction, by far the easiest route there would be over water. Somewhat obviously care had to be taken to ensure the steam packet they had borrowed drew no more water than the boat which would have made the same voyage had it not been sunk, but that being so the journey could be made in safety.

There was, of course, the question of why the steam packet had to be borrowed when it might have been supposed that the police themselves would have such a vessel. There being no argument that the police in the dock area at least would have found one to be invaluable. It is, of course, ever thus. In this country of ours it seems the forces of the law must forever wait on the advances our science gives us. Apparently their lot is to be always behind the rest of our society and, scandalously, also behind the criminal element.

Facts that Inspector Allaby presumably knew, but was not disposed to mention as he conversed with Doyle. His thoughts being on matters of much more personal concern, as Doyle was to discover.

"Should make a good story, this," the inspector began by way of broaching the subject. "A *Penny Dreadful* as well unless I miss my mark."

At this Doyle chuckled. "Your aim is true," he told the inspector. "I am intending to publish a novelette, providing it can have a satisfactory ending."

He could also have said that he intended his work to be of a superior quality to those overly sentimental and lurid sheets generally referred to as *Penny Dreadfuls* although in this instance he refrained. Now was not the time for a discussion on literary merit, especially when the inspector so obviously had other thoughts on his mind. As proven by his next comment, made after a slow nod of his head to show he understood the importance of a satisfactory conclusion.

"A story such as this would have many characters," he began, his words chosen carefully. "Some more important than others."

"As you say," Doyle agreed, beginning to see the direction this conversation was taking, a suspicion knowingly confirmed by the inspector.

"Some would even be more prominent than others," he continued, his intention now obvious.

"Naturally so," Doyle once again agreed. "In every story there will always be a character of greater importance than others. In this story, as I see it, that would have to be the policeman who led the investigation to its successful finish."

Then, that said, the two men looked at each other in perfect understanding. Being ambitious, as he was, the inspector was anxious to know how he would be portrayed when Doyle wrote his story. A good account and his reputation would be enhanced which would be all to the good when it came to the matter of his advancement. A bad account, of course, would leave his career beached.

It was to his good fortune then that Doyle understood all of this. The more so as he had done nothing to make Doyle question his competence or his integrity and was, therefore, well disposed towards the man. A fact that was made clear, if unspoken, when the two looked at each other, the both of them knowing no more need be said.

A statement which was, in fact, observed. For the remainder of the journey they spoke very little and even then more out of proximity than desire for speech. In the main the inspector spoke with his men leaving Doyle free to look out at the city. The place that was both his home and his livelihood now passed by on either side of the river.

Either by chance or design the steam packet borrowed for the occasion had a tall, almost elongated, funnel which kept the smoke well away from its occupants. Doyle was thus able to stand at the prow and enjoy as clear a view of the city as the early morning mist would allow. From the great ships at berth in the docks, the starting point of their journey, to the warehouses and factories beyond them it was all laid out before him. Even the bridge with its dark memories stood innocently in the pale sun. The early train crossing it seemingly a symbol of how far Man had conquered nature.

Through there, as the boat chugged up the river, industry in the form of grey factories and mills gave way to the demands of housing. Mean tenement blocks now appeared; residences for those who worked in the self-same factories. Their lowly status confirmed by their very location for who else would live by that dark, oft foul smelling water. Only those whose choice was denied by poverty.

It was also those same tenement blocks which could be said to mark the city boundary as beyond them, bare fields became greener and the water ever clearer, the dirt of the city giving way to the freshness of nature. Soon that was all that could be seen as the city lay far behind them and the boat continued on its way through what was almost a rustic idyll. Fields unchanged for centuries lay dormant in the early morning mist, the frost still about them.

Of course, before long that too changed. The marsh now started to appear. Itself a sign they were nearing the end of their journey which, as they soon discovered, was to be the case. Ahead of them, taking form slowly through the mist, an ugly, squat, grey building began to appear. Longer than it was broad and seemingly devoid of windows its very form seemed to shriek its purpose. No-one who saw it could ever believe it was a place where acts of goodness were performed. On the contrary, the place was evil. It had that air.

To the surprise of no-one it was also their destination. The steam packet took them inexorably closer to the stone-built quay immediately in front of the building. As it did so a singular series of events occurred which, as Doyle would soon learn, was all part of a carefully laid plan.

The first he knew of it was when uniformed police appeared around the building.

"Telegraphed ahead," Inspector Allaby muttered by way of explaining their presence.

At the sound of their engine approaching a door at the front of the building opened, those inside presumably curious about what it could be. After that all was consternation. On seeing the boat with its uniformed figures on board the man at the door turned to shout something inaudible to those approaching, but which could only be a warning before he took flight. A second man now appeared at the door also intending to flee. The both of them were looking to make their escape which would have happened but for the police there waiting for them.

A neat trap in which both were held to the obvious delight of the inspector whose smile of triumph needed no further comment.

"My congratulations," Doyle murmured in praise of such farsightedness, making the inspector smile even more.

It was, then, with great good humour that he left the boat to take stock of the two who were now his prisoners. Aged and thin with as few teeth as they apparently had scruples, they were indeed miserable specimens of humanity. There as gatekeepers, watchers perhaps, for what other function could they perform? Naught else could be entrusted to them.

This realisation did much to remove the smile from the face of Inspector Allaby. Hoping for big game he had merely caught two sprats, worthless to him or the investigation. A galling fact made all the worse by the thought that, as only they had appeared, the building itself must now be empty. In which case there would be few prizes to be had inside.

Indeed, as far as they knew, the place might even be bare. In itself a sobering thought and yet one which had to be faced. They could have made a fruitless journey. The truth of which they would only know once they entered the building, as they now prepared to do.

Leaving his prisoners with the uniformed constabulary outside, Inspector Allaby led the way, followed by the rest of his men with Doyle bringing up the rear. A position he took not because of some police regulation that consigned him there, in fact no mention was made of any regulations or rules.

Rather he was in the rear because as he left the boat he glanced up to see a sight which made him pause for a moment.

His actions in this unremarked by the police who simply moved past him on their way into the building which was why only Doyle saw it. For that matter only Doyle would have understood the significance so there was no loss. A benefit quite possibly as it saved an uncomfortable explanation and so Doyle made no complaint where none was needed. In truth he gave it no thought as he continued to stare into the sky.

His eyes not on the sky as such, but on the ravens, many of them. Silently they flew overhead to land on the roof of that same building. Equally silent they perched there, staring down at the humans beneath them. To Doyle this was a heartening sight. As he saw it, they would hardly be there just to observe the disappointment and discomfort of the police. The only conclusion possible was that the building still held secrets; something worthwhile was still to be found. For which reason he hurried after the police to join them in that place of murder. That gloomy place of evil.

With light coming only from two grimy skylights the police had been forced to search for lanterns by whose light they could now inspect the building. Their shadows flickered over packing cases and walls to lend the place a thoroughly ghastly air, an unearthly air, most definitely in keeping with its history.

Yet it has to be said if that same history had been unknown far fewer ghosts would have been seen. Certainly, there was nothing immediately visible to suggest its nefarious past. In one part of what was a large chamber stood a table and some chairs. Empty bottles on and beside the table provided evidence of its usage. In various places crates, some of tobacco and some of liquor, were stacked against walls. Contraband beyond doubt, but by no means a prize of any significance.

In one corner a dark stain on the floor, improperly cleaned and still with traces of sawdust, clearly marked the spot where Joseph Malloy had met his end. Grisly enough it has to be admitted, and not for those of an overly delicate nature, although it was expected. Its value, therefore, only as confirmation that such an event had happened, that the testimony of their witnesses was true. Essential to the legal mind perhaps, but no more.

"Our prize has eluded us," Inspector Allaby muttered dejectedly.

An opinion apparently shared by all, with the exception of Doyle. Knowing the significance of the ravens, as he did, only he was prepared to continue the search. At first by examining the crates and cases more closely on the chance that their labels gave the lie to the contents. A search that earned him only the bemused looks of his police companions.

Unabashed he continued. His gaze now on the floor, his faith in the ravens secure. Soon more than secure, vindicated. He found what he could only believe he was intended to find.

"A light," he asked, the floor being mainly in shadow.

A lantern soon being made available he could now see where two holes, worn and much used, had been drilled into a wooden floor beam. Of themselves not suspicious until he cast his eyes around the near vicinity to find what he knew would be there. A hook, thick and solid with wide handle, propped up against the wall by the side of some packing cases.

With a satisfied sigh he took hold of it, knowing it would fit into those drilled holes. He pulled on the handle to feel it move barely an inch or two, his efforts enough to show the outlines of a trapdoor, but not sufficient to open it.

At a sign from the inspector a constable stepped forward, adding his strength to Doyle's. The two of them now able to raise the trapdoor, they revealed what lay beneath. Surely the prize foreshadowed by the ravens was now within their grasp; the secret of that dark building about to be discovered.

With a cry of, "Well done, that man!" the inspector stepped forward only to stop short as a fetid odour reached him. A smell not of the farm, but of the cesspit, rank and foul. Soon it reached them all, threatening to overpower them until some unnamed individual opened the outside door so it could be dispersed by the fresh morning air. Not a moment too soon in the opinion of all.

Even so it lingered, the foulness still there as the inspector shone a lantern through the trapdoor into whatever was the cause of such malodour. Its beam penetrated the dark to show wooden steps leading down.

Steeling himself, the inspector stepped forward again until he stood at the very top of those stairs, the lantern beam now reaching to the floor beneath. By its light he saw a bucket, filth, some rags. As yet there was no hint of what creature lurked below until, that is, the inspector heard a sound, something moving in the darkness.

The light turned on it he saw to his surprise, and his horror, it was no creature of the wild but men, two of them. Cowering back against the wall, obviously fearing the worst, they could only stare up at him, defenceless as they were. It was they who were the secret of that building. Its purpose now seen to be not a place of storage, but of incarceration.

As to what crimes, if crimes they were, had been committed by such sorry individuals was the question now to be answered. Accordingly the inspector made it clear they could leave the cellar dungeon, this done more by wave of arm than spoken word, an action which was at first ignored. Those men, the prisoners, too wary of strangers to obey even unspoken commands.

Only the sight of police uniforms roused them from their dread, enough at least for them to hesitantly climb the stairs so they could be seen by all. Objects of curiosity indeed, but also of pity. Of that there could be no mistake.

One swarthy of skin and the other much darker they were as much different as they were alike. Both casting fearful, mistrusting looks about them which told of their rough treatment. Both also in rags, torn and dirty. Yet beyond that they seemed to be as much strangers to each other as they were to the police. Even the language they each spoke was different.

Foreign beyond a doubt and so unintelligible to all there, including each other, so it seemed. Certainly, when one spoke in his own tongue the other gave no sign of understanding. Their connection, then, only that they shared the same dungeon. Who they were, or the reason for them being there, as much a mystery to each other as it was to the police.

On that score only deduction was available. Having given up all attempts at communication Inspector Allaby paused to assess the situation.

"Not part of the gang we came for," he muttered, shaking his head as he did so. "Otherwise there would have been no imprisonment for them. They would have met the same end as Joseph Malloy."

"Waiting to be bought like a side of beef," Doyle muttered in agreement.

And with that thought, all became clear to him. Elijah Jackson and his ilk had an acquaintance with those of the medical profession because they were suppliers to that particular trade. The prisoners were no more than livestock; animals to be kept until a price had been agreed. Then they would be butchered with as much compunction as a farmer sending his cows to the slaughterhouse.

He looked at the face of Inspector Allaby and received confirmation of his belief, saw the same thought reflected back at him.

A filthy trade as the man had once called it, an ungodly trade, yet in no other way could the facts be reconciled. Resurrection men were abroad once again, murdering then selling bodies to the medical profession. An ungodly trade as it had once been now it was something far worse. Now the trade was murderous.

Chapter Twelve

Explanations and Admiration

"We finally discovered one came from West Africa, the other from the East Indies," Doyle told his audience of but two – Canon Jeffries and Miss Burton. "And that only after much effort. Having brought them back with us on the steam packet we could do no more than tour the great ships currently in port until we found people who recognised their tongue although, unfortunately, not the individuals. Nevertheless, a Boson in one case and a Captain in another were kind enough to speak to the men on our behalf so we could be told their story." Here he shook his head sadly as if at the thought of it. Their story being best described as pathetic in its simplicity. "Deck hands both," he continued, "they sailed on ships from their own countries which brought them here. Then, while ashore, they were separately attacked and bound before being taken to that building where they were kept. They also told of others there like them who had already been taken away."

As a result of this, Canon Jefferies shuddered slightly in full appreciation of that significance, indeed in full understanding of it all. The monstrous tale was easily followed. In such a cosmopolitan city great ships regularly arrived from all parts of the Empire and beyond, their cargoes being much sought after. In like manner their crews also arrived and just as often failed to return. That being so commonplace no search was made for them, nor was it felt necessary to inform the police. They simply vanished, usually for their own reasons which was most often a better berth on a different ship, but which it seemed could also be for reasons more foul. Those who would never be missed were taken for the profit of others.

"Devilry," the canon breathed before giving Doyle a curious look. "Where are they now?"

"Now being cared for in a Seaman's Mission while legal matters are being attended to," he answered before giving a slight smile. "According to a plaque on the wall the trustees of that include a certain Mr Jacob Arthan."

The irony of that not being lost on the canon he too smiled slightly.

"The bible tells us that in all things God works for the good of those who love Him," he answered, looking straight at Doyle. "So it would seem that by your hand this day God's work has been done."

"Hardly just my hand," Doyle murmured in reply. There were, after all, many hands involved of which he was just one.

"But yours did the most part of it," Miss Burton told him, admiration in her gaze.

As true as that was, he had indeed played a major role, nevertheless Doyle should perhaps have protested more. In that he fell silent, his only defence being the perfectly natural desire to bask in her admiration as any man would. Such an occasion was to be savoured as all those who have ever been in love will readily attest.

Miss Burton's presence there was by his hand although in this case he was guilty of some slight subterfuge. While it was true he had written her a note the substance of which was the crisis recently faced by the canon and a suggestion she might care to call on him to ensure his continued wellbeing he did so not just for the sake of the canon. His motives were far more personal. As he reasoned, if she was there when he happened to call on the man as he now did with some regularity then what better way to further their relationship. It being unseemly for him to call on here at her home.

For her part it should be said Miss Burton at once understood the true meaning of the note; feminine wisdom winning out as ever in the face of masculine folly. However, she still elected to follow his suggestion for reasons strikingly similar to his own. A fact of which Doyle would be forever ignorant.

His thoughts regarding her at that moment being the tenderness created when she displayed that understanding which is the very essence of her gender by divining the two men wished to talk alone and so offered to make arrangements for tea to be served. Her soft smile as she did so proof she knew the effect of her actions on the already ensnared Doyle.

A more worldly man than the canon might have remarked on this, would certainly have praised her suitability for a wife, but much as he indeed admired her the canon was too pre-occupied with other thoughts, his mind at that moment dwelling only on their previous encounter and his condition during it.

"It seemed I must offer you my apologies, and my thanks," he mumbled, unable to look Doyle in the eye so great was his embarrassment.

"You need offer me neither," the other answered gently.

Words that produced but silence from the canon. It was ever thus, of course. When faced with matters of a personal nature even the most eloquent of us can be unable to find their tongue.

"I was weak," he spoke again. His words soft, but growing in power as he continued. "That is how the devil works. He finds our weaknesses and uses them against us."

At this Doyle stirred uneasily, and for good reason. Amongst gentlemen such conversations would always be uncomfortable. Nevertheless, he felt compelled to reply.

"It was your compassion at work and that should never be seen as a weakness."

The truth of this being so self-evident the canon could only nod, once again mollified by the words of the other although, strangely, this time he felt no sense of indebtedness. Doyle had merely stated what, in his heart, he already knew to be correct. Even so he felt a certain gratitude towards the man for expressing it so that, now being openly addressed, it could be dealt with. By this, of course, it is meant the subject would be talked of no more. That being the way such gentlemen handle these matters. A fact signified by the canon becoming brisker, more business-like, as he looked at Doyle.

"I believe it is time to strike back at the devil," he announced. "And your tale has shown me how it may be done."

This being much of a surprise to Doyle, he could only stare until the canon explained further.

"If your guess is right, and I believe it to be so, then many will have met their end in such way, leaving their souls unshriven." Here he stopped so there was no mistaking what in different eyes would have been anger. Even so in his eyes steel had appeared. "The helpless taken captive and then despatched in such a manner for the profit of others," he continued, steel now also in his voice, "it strains the mercy of man and provides tasty morsels for the devil, but no more. He shall not keep them."

The voice of the canon having risen in defiance now fell to an altogether softer tone, yet determined still.

"It is my intention to perform a service within the church for those wretched souls as were taken before their time. With the help of the Almighty I shall wrest them from the clutches of the devil so they may finally feel the grace of God."

As Doyle had once before discovered in these situations his compassion, nay his faith, shone through so that the only answer possible was to simply bow his head. The traditional mark of respect.

"Will that be an end to it?" he asked, thinking of the darkness at the bridge.

"Alas no," the canon answered. "Greater forces were at work there of which we still have no knowledge. In God's good time we may come to know of it, but until then this will be merely an act of defiance, or charity perhaps."

An act of goodness to set against the wickedness they had recently encountered as it could also be described. Its effectiveness unknown, but that would be no bar to its execution. After all, with souls at stake the canon could be expected to do no less.

On that he was not bidden by ravens, but by his God.

CHAPTER THIRTEEN

OF PLANS LAID

If the status of an individual be determined in some part by his surroundings, or the surroundings to which he is invited, then Doyle could say his stock had lately risen. The proof of it was in the elegance of the establishment which he was now entering. This was no mere ale house and while it was true there were other places which served a much more affluent clientele nevertheless this was not the haunt of those involved in manual labour. Rather it was a place for those who looked to be better; who aspired to be better.

Those people amongst whose ranks Inspector Allaby was firmly listed. He being the person who had invited Doyle to meet him there so further actions could be planned in their hunt for the elusive, and unnamed, individual whom they now knew to be the murderer of Joseph Malloy quite apart from his other crimes. A most wanted man as he could be described and yet still anonymous. Despite all their efforts, discussions and interviews with his gang members they were still no closer to even learning his name, far less making an arrest.

The very reason why Doyle had received his invitation. In

the words of the inspector a plan of campaign was called for and his contribution would be much valued. Both the charitable, and admittedly immodest, side of Doyle liked to think this was in recognition of his previous efforts although it has to be said he knew better. A more sober assessment had it the inspector was anxious of his reputation which would be made or marred when Doyle wrote his novelette. Reason enough for him to extend every courtesy in the hope of future return.

Be that as it may Doyle was there in the company of both inspectors so matters could be discussed while they warmed themselves with glasses of mulled wine; the surroundings convivial if not the conversation. That at first was far from convivial; Inspector Marchant setting the tone with the single word: "Nothing."

He was, of course, referring to how much they knew about their quarry which, by the tone in which he said it, was obviously a source of great frustration.

By way of doing justice to the inspector it should be said at that moment he was not well disposed. The main cause of which being the coat he was still wearing, or, more precisely, the fact that he was obliged to keep wearing it to hide his uniform underneath. The management of this particular establishment apparently not being happy at the sight of a police uniform no matter what the rank of its occupant. As an aside it did point to which of the two inspectors had chosen the place of their meeting which was confirmed by the look the one occasionally gave the other. Clearly he was not happy with the arrangement.

As for Inspector Allaby, while he did offer a conciliatory glance or two, on the whole his manner was indifferent. As far as he was concerned they were there, at a place of his choosing, to discuss a matter of pressing importance and let that be an end to it. An opinion he showed by taking note of what was said while ignoring the manner of it.

"Therefore, we must look for ways of conjuring up something out of nothing," he said calmly.

At which, both inspectors sat back. The one to show he was opening up the discussion to the floor, as it might be so described, and the other to show he had no suggestion to make. The pair of them creating a silence into which Doyle ventured, feeling he had no choice in the matter.

"Have you heard mention of a Jacob Arthan?" he asked quietly, looking at neither of the inspectors.

It was a question he almost feared to ask and yet its effect was immediate. As one, both inspectors leaned forward, their faces serious.

"And when would you have heard of him?" Inspector Allaby asked softly, but with grim intent.

"It was pointed out to me," Doyle could only answer, failing to mention his informant in this had dark feathers and wings.

"Your sources are good," Inspector Allaby told him, looking impressed despite himself. "But yes. We have often wondered at the nature of that man's wealth."

"But with no solid reason to investigate him," Inspector Marchant added.

Here Doyle nodded slowly. Mentioning the name had been an act almost of desperation. A throw of the dice as it were. Not knowing how it would be received he had done it only because no other option was on offer, the inspectors seemingly stymied. For which reason he felt justified in taking what was only a slight risk as a means of introducing another consideration not yet mentioned.

It was, therefore, to his relief that he discovered Jacob Arthan was known to them. Not as a suspect, if that be the correct term, but definitely someone of whom they had suspicions. A person who had attracted their interest as it could probably be best described. An interest that was now more than a little piqued, thanks to Doyle.

"Now you mention the name," Inspector Allaby said slowly, "for what reason?"

Here Doyle knew his words must be chosen carefully.

"It was while thinking of that boat being loaded with contraband. The one sank by Joseph Malloy. That was when it occurred to me the contraband must have been stored somewhere else first. It would hardly have been left out for all to see. If that be the case then where else but in one of the warehouses further along the quay from where the police and excisemen were watching."

At his words smiles of understanding appeared on the faces of both inspectors.

"One of the warehouses close by," Inspector Marchant breathed.

"The owners of which can easily be found," Inspector Allaby sighed.

"And I happen to know one of those belongs to Jacob Arthan," Doyle added to complete their delight.

Beyond doubt the apprehension of such a man would be

an achievement to savour. Their reputations assured by it. Advancement also perhaps, although first they had to be sure of their catch as the ever pragmatic Inspector Marchant made clear. Now was not the time to go rushing about blindly.

"Best be sure of him first," he muttered. "We need to be certain."

"Wise words." Inspector Allaby nodded in agreement, for the moment prepared to heed the advice of the other. "There can be two, at most three, warehouses that fit the bill. We must investigate the owners of each and if one happens to be Jacob Arthan then so be it."

As he spoke a smile of slow satisfaction began to spread across his face. As the unknown and still unnamed chief, the murderer they were hunting, was reported to be of superior status to the rogues still in their custody surely it would be he who owned the warehouse. How else to maintain a law abiding façade. In which case, if Inspector Allaby was accurate in his reckoning, they had at best three names to consider. One of them was their man. Even more enticingly one of the names was Jacob Arthan.

"With him under lock and key the hold he has over the rest of his gang will be broken," the inspector said, smiling even more. "After which if just one of them is prepared to testify, his journey to the gallows is guaranteed."

"But first we must place him under lock and key," Inspector Marchant reminded him. "There is no crime in owning a warehouse, or must we arrest all three."

His words, solid and practical as they were, produced only silence. Their only other effect being to erase Inspector

Allaby's smile. A fact which if it caused some slight satisfaction in the man sitting uncomfortably in his overcoat would have been nothing but human.

As would the chagrin when the inspector rose to the challenge.

"We must lay our plans carefully," he answered after reasonable thought. "First we must find out more about these warehouse owners. After that, assuming Jacob Arthan being the only one suitable which I believe we will find, then we make our move."

At this point the other two men in the company both noticed the smile had come back on his face. This time, however, it was not a smile of satisfaction. It was the thrill of the chase.

"It occurs to me," he continued, "that with no place left to store any contraband for lengthy periods, without even a boat to ferry it there, any recent deliveries must still be held in his warehouse."

"If there have been any deliveries recently," Inspector Marchant felt compelled to remind him.

"Which I believe there must have been," the other replied, the first flush of enthusiasm showing on his face. "Keep in mind there was a large place of storage to keep it hidden and a boat to move it there. That speaks to many deliveries of great quantity. Furthermore, as they could never contact the ships at sea carrying that contraband here they would still arrive and expect it to be unloaded and paid for."

He smiled again, this time a smile of confidence.

"That is how it will be done," he continued, each word

slow and deliberate. "A search of the warehouse will reveal the contraband and then we have him."

"*If* it's there," Inspector Marchant said again. "That's a mighty big gamble."

True words, but not enough to deflect the other who sat straight in his chair, decision taken.

"A wager I'm prepared to make," he said with finality.

They would do it, he would do it, but as to the outcome no-one could say for sure. That belonged to a higher power. A power not of this world who saw all and judged all. A power into which, unknowingly, the success or otherwise of their plan had just been placed.

As for the rest, that greater mystery, it too was in the hands of a higher power. The resolution of it depending on more than just ravens. As time would tell its untangling would be the work of many, with the church being not the least part of it.

Chapter Fourteen

Searches and Discoveries

It was a bleak day, a dark day. A day when it almost seemed as if the very heavens were at war; dark clouds gathering to seed the gusting wind with flecks of snow. The sun hidden behind those same clouds providing neither light nor heat. A day, in fact, when no creature of this world should have been abroad. Such a day was not for them.

Certainly, it was no day to be standing on a quay by the river, exposed to the snow and the wind, which all those present were in full agreement. But for the overriding call of duty they would have happily been elsewhere. The exact location immaterial just as long as it involved shelter from the biting wind and a fire to ward off the cold. A pot or two of ale would also be welcome.

With such thoughts do men keep themselves insulated. In this case as they stood on that quay prior to effecting entry to the warehouses opposite, that being the purpose in being there. A fact from which it will be readily deduced that the men in question were the police. The presence of Doyle also being an easy guess to make. Not such an easy guess, although certainly true, was the presence of the excisemen. There because contraband fell under their responsibility. Their jurisdiction as it is understood was the correct term.

That notwithstanding there were far fewer present than Doyle expected. The number available seemingly insufficient for the searching of what was in fact three warehouses. Apparently Inspector Allaby had been right in his estimate.

For the rest of it as far as Doyle could make out he had been denied more people because of the speculative nature of this undertaking. With the resources of the police perpetually stretched, as they were, no more could be spared without dislocating other activities just as important. For such reason the decision was made which, to his credit, Inspector Allaby understood and made little complaint although it has to be said the result was far from satisfactory, to him at least.

On that score perhaps it should be said the real culprit here was not the senior officers who denied him the resources, but the fact that adequate resources were denied them. With too few for the immense task they were charged with they could only take such decisions and trust to the zeal, and inventiveness, of their subordinates. Facts which were well known and yet still ignored for which we must all plead guilty. The blame lay elsewhere, not with the police.

Yet it was a still the police who were forced to make do with whatever scant resources they were given. In this case by taking the decision not to enter all of the warehouses at the same time as would have been preferred. Instead, all available men would be used to search one warehouse before moving on to another. A compromise at best, as all had to agree, and one which would prolong the business well into the afternoon, but for which there was no other choice. Necessity forced them to it.

Accordingly they trooped into the first of the warehouses to be inspected. An establishment owned by an affable personage with the name of Saunders who raised no objection and positively welcomed them in. His motto in life, and in business, seeming to be: enough, but no more. This was not a man of overarching ambition.

As they soon discovered, this was also how he organised his affairs. His business, presumably, providing him with a respectable living he saw no reason for further work, or to scrutinise every penny and every transaction. To the staff no doubt a providential employer for that very reason although the police and the excisemen found themselves taking a different view. There were a host of discrepancies in his accounts and his inventory which, while time consuming, could never be considered serious. He was not their man.

That being the case, after fruitless hours had passed, they left him with a few stern words from the excisemen and a promise of reform from him which both sides knew would be ignored. For him bonhomie would always be a substitute for efficiency. Unlike the next warehouse they visited. This was under the control of a Mr Isaacs who claimed he was an agent acting on behalf of the owner much to the surprise of Inspector Allaby who had never heard of such a thing. Judging by the looks on the faces of the excisemen they too were not familiar with this type of arrangement although this they tried to hide, presumably for the sake of some rivalry or other between them and the police.

Nevertheless, it must be said Mr Isaacs was a more than competent manager. From the cleanliness of the floor to the accuracy of the accounting the place was the very epitome of efficiency. A credit to its manager and an easy task for the police and excisemen who needed no time to declare the place free of contraband. Neither Mr Isaacs nor the missing owner was their man.

That, therefore, left just the one to search. The one they were really interested in.

"Best till last," Inspector Allaby muttered as he led the way to the door of the warehouse owned by Jacob Arthan. There to be met not by the man himself, but by a sullen individual who tried to bar his entry. The courage for this coming from three surly labourers who also stood behind the door.

"Private property," the sullen one told the inspector. "Needs permission before you can come in here."

"That I have," the inspector told him, patting his breast pocket. "From the courts themselves."

If he was astonished at such a brazen attitude it was as nothing compared to his reaction when the sullen one simply held his hand out, demanding the court documents be handed over. To him!

"I'll not tarry here with you," the inspector exclaimed indignantly. "I'll serve them to the owner and if he's not here I'll serve them later. Now out of my way."

At this, with impudence beyond words, the sullen one moved to stand full square in the doorway, the labourers moving in close behind him. Obviously expecting the inspector to try and push by they stood ready to block his path only to find he was a thought ahead of them. Rather than stepping forward he stepped aside, gesturing to the uniformed police behind him who stood with truncheons drawn. They it was who marched forward with a determined look that said cross us if you dare. We are the law.

A step or two was all it took. Determined men with a purpose, and with right on their side, faced those whose bravado soon failed as it only could. Outmatched they stood, they hesitated, then they turned and ran. The entrance to the warehouse was now clear, the fact of it marked by the ribald cheers and jeers of those standing beside it.

A moral victory only, but a victory all the same. Just what was needed to raise the spirits of the men and give encouragement to the inspector who reasoned there must be something worth finding if they would go to such lengths to keep him from it. Therefore, and again as he reasoned, he would soon have his man, not to mention his vindication.

For that reason it was with high hopes he entered the warehouse proper even if what he might find there was still beyond his guess. Although he was by now certain it would not include Jacob Arthan he was, nevertheless, sure he would find something noteworthy. If not enough to hang the man then at least enough to arrest him as a means of breaking his power. A more than satisfactory conclusion in police eyes.

Even so first of all he had to find the evidence, whatever it might be. A task made no easier by the sullen and surly nature of those employees as worked inside the warehouse. Not for them the cheerful bumbling or the calm efficiency encountered at the previous establishments. They openly resented the official presence and were unhelpful to the point of obstruction. At times beyond even that.

Indeed, it seemed as if their attitude was deliberately calculated to annoy the inspector whose irritation increased as time wore on with no sign of any illicit activity. The warehouse seemed to be free of contraband, at least as far as they could tell. The place was by no means easy to search. Whether by accident or design the entire warehouse, and a big warehouse at that, was filled with cases, stacked high and with very little space between them. A high inventory to be sure and yet all of it legitimate.

Eventually, to his frustration, Inspector Allaby had to admit there was nothing to be found. His mood was made all the darker by the sneers of the warehouse staff so obviously enjoying his discomfiture. It also has to be said the excisemen did little to alleviate the situation although their smiles were more of self-satisfaction than denigration. Their experience in these matters being greater than that of the police, they were more aware of the ruses employed by those who traded in contraband, one of which they eventually decided to share.

After leaving the inspector to squirm on what was a rack of his own making long enough to make whatever point they intended to make, one of them, presumably the man in charge, relented. With a half smile and a gesture of the head he indicated that the inspector should follow him to where his own men were already dismantling two stacks of crates. That done the way was clear to yet more crates stacked behind them. On dismantling those stacks other, different, boxes were revealed hidden behind them. Boxes that conspicuously lacked the Revenue stamp. Contraband in other words.

"A common trick," the exciseman told the inspector whose incredulous look spoke volumes. "Surround the illegal with regular goods and block the way with yet more. Keeps them safe from most eyes, even those that are looking." Here he shook his head just the once as if to acknowledge the compromise involved when he added. "Does make them difficult to get at though."

"Which would be why the other place of storage was needed," Doyle added as he saw the sense of it all. "That way they could be reached without delay."

"Just so," the exciseman agreed, giving Doyle a thoughtful look.

They had been introduced, but by name only. No mention had been made of his status or his purpose in being there. The reason why, perhaps, being obvious to the reader, but not so to Inspector of Excise Perkins, to give the man both his title and his name. Now, presumably because he considered he had earned their trust, he felt entitled to ask more, the question forming on his lips when they were interrupted by the crashing sound of a door being flung open.

As intrusive as it was unexpected, they started, then turned as one to seek out its cause. A task made easier due to its constant repetition. Their search guided by the sound of it, not to mention a sudden icy draft, it took no time to discover the source as being a door now crashing repeatedly against its jamb.

"The means by which someone left in haste," Inspector Allaby muttered, stating what was surely obvious.

Had anyone entered that way they would have naturally barred the door behind them, if only to keep out the bitter cold and flurries of snow. Therefore, there being no other option, someone must have left through it and in such a hurry they neglected to fasten the door behind them. Hardly the greatest deduction then, and yet it provided explanation for what had happened at least. The who and why, of course, remained unanswered.

As to that no-one had a guess, not even Doyle who could only shrug when both police and excisemen turned towards him as if he could somehow divine more than they. It was as much of a mystery to him. That being the case he could do no more than watch as Inspector Appleby turned it to the good, just as he had done on a previous occasion.

"It's alerted us to the door at any rate," he told all those assembled there. "So now we can make sure it's guarded."

Despite its origin the point was still well made. Hidden as it was behind packing cases tightly stacked together the none of them knew it was there. Now, of course, after it had been revealed it could be guarded to prevent the escape of those warehouse employees who would soon have cause to regret their recent attitude. Indeed, would soon have cause to regret their very employment in that place. As they were about to find out the law could be unforgiving.

A truth which was soon implanted on the faces of all concerned. The warehouse employees all looked downcast and resentful although whether it was the police who arrested them or their employer who implicated them that was the cause of their resentment had yet to be determined. Most likely it was a combination of both. As for the police their motives were as obvious as the grins on their faces when they performed the arrests, and who could blame them.

At that moment the law was ascendant, as proved not just by the arrests, but by the impressive amount of contraband they eventually impounded. More than enough for the excisemen to consider it a job well done and leave everything else to the police who were still feeling dissatisfied. The most part of this, of course, coming from the lack of that one arrest they wanted most of all: Jacob Arthan. His still being at large was a fact they felt all too keenly to such an extent they actually begrudged the time spent collecting and cataloguing his illicit goods. They should have been after him instead was the opinion of them all.

Nevertheless, as with most things, that came to an end and they were able to leave the warehouse to find a bleak afternoon rapidly turning into a worse evening. The kind of evening when it was easy to believe dark forces were abroad. The clouds thick and menacing. The wind carrying not just flecks of snow, but also a wail as of souls in torment. Their distant cries mingling with the crunch of boots on the thick frost already forming.

A wild night, then, and yet a night when they were committed to being out of doors. Their choice dictated by duty. Not for them the warm comfort of their own fireside. Instead, they must be about their business which, that evening, was the apprehension of Jacob Arthan, wherever he might be.

A question that occupied them all, not the least Inspector Allaby, who as yet had nothing to guide him even though he would soon need to give his orders, as he well knew. For the moment he was able to put off that event by helping with the general confusion as the excisemen summoned carts and prepared the recently discovered contraband to be taken to their own premises. Once that was done, however, he knew all would be looking to him; his need for an answer becoming pressing. Indeed, becoming urgent until, that is, a youth surely too young to be in the police arrived, seeking out the inspector through the bustle of the crowd. His face flushed as proof of his exertion he found his man and handed over a note he had obviously come to deliver. Then, once a coin changed hands, he was gone, his mission served.

As for the inspector he glanced at the note, realised it was too dark to read its contents, and took himself back into the light of the warehouse. On his return there was no mistaking his smile of triumph and, no doubt, relief.

"I had my spies watching the house of that man Arthan," he began by way of explanation. "They report a man arrived looking for all the world as if he had run all the way there. Doubtless the same one who left here in haste just after the illicit stock was discovered. At a guess that was his purpose. To provide warning the game was up."

Here the inspector looked around for those who would argue and found no dissent. In this his analysis was accepted. As they all agreed, it was only sensible for Jacob Arthan to take such a precaution; waiting to see if his illegal activities had been discovered. If not he would, of course, carry on, but if they were a runner was on hand to inform him straight away. The better to make his escape.

"My report has it he immediately went to the bank where

it is believed he withdrew a large amount of money. He was then seen returning home, no doubt making preparations to flee. We must hurry to catch him," he continued. "Come. The chase is up."

They were about to start a wild venture on a wild night, but could it be, was the end finally in sight? Or had this tale more to offer. A question only the night could answer. On this occasion no-one needed to ask the ravens, nor were they there to be questioned.

They were elsewhere. Their reasons unknown, as was their precise location. Nerveless, as Doyle at least knew they would return, and they would be needed.

CHAPTER FIFTEEN

SERMONS AND SÉANCES

As events were to unfold on that dark and stormy night many others were also involved. Their motives different. Their locations also different and yet each was destined to play a part in such proceedings, fragmented as they were, which constitute the next part of this tale. A fabric in which several strands must be woven together.

For which reason we must leave Doyle and the police hurrying on their way to the city residence of Jacob Arthan and turn our attention instead to the home of Madame Clara. There to find preparations in hand for the séance she was intending to perform that evening. The clairvoyant, it seemed, had either decided not to take any notice of Doyle or else had seen his warning for the theatrics it mainly was. Not that the issue was worth discussing further. For all practical purposes the only point worthy of consideration was that she intended to conduct a séance. The reasons why immaterial.

Nevertheless, that was not to say she totally discounted the warning given to her by Doyle. In fact she took it to heart so that on this occasion her guests included none of her usual clientele. Rather she had gathered fellow mystics both for their support and for their subjugation. If her plans worked through, that evening she intended to emerge as pre-eminent amongst them.

Accordingly, then, she addressed them before any such proceedings began. That being her way of setting the scene if it could be so described.

"Fellow practitioners," she began as a means of calling to order what had been until then a varied mix of conversation, gossip and rumour mongering as was found whenever likeminded individuals were gathered together. "Let me explain our purpose for this evening. I have been informed by one who is in a position to know of elemental forces disturbing the spirit world. Of the cause higher powers will not allow me to disclose even to you, my friends. All I can say is I have been charged with using my gifts to seek out those troubled spirits so that they may know peace once more." At this point she paused to look around her as a means of adding weight to her, more than partly fabricated, tale and also to what was about to come next.

"In this my duty is clear," she informed them in tones full of meaning. "To join with me on this I turn to you, my colleagues. My Camelot."

That last spoken with even more meaning to leave no-one there in any doubt. In this she intended to be the queen, a female Arthur. They to be her subjects; equal unto themselves, but with her dominant over them.

The announcement, nay the revelation, coming as more than a little of a surprise to her guests there was as might be imagined a certain amount of consternation. This was not to their liking, nor was it the reason why they came.

Facts which were soon made clear.

"You said this was to be a gathering to our mutual advantage," the sole male psychic in the room reminded her in a thick accent. "In what way will this be to our advantage?"

This was the man who styled himself as Gregori Von Hollingburg or Count Schulman as was shown on his business cards. A tall, thin, individual who claimed to be descended from a liaison between an Eastern European Countess, to explain the title, and a Romany prince, from where his psychic powers were derived. The exact truth of the matter being difficult to verify.

He was, nevertheless, of aristocratic bearing and dress which made him an unlikely servant. Even less did it make him a follower as Madame Clara was quick to acknowledge.

"When I invited you all here to our mutual advantage I was sincere," she told him calmly. "How else could it be otherwise if we assist the spirits?"

Phrased as it was the question could have only one answer yet even that she forestalled with a smile that was both soft and innocent.

"Enough of this," she continued, addressing them all. "Come. Let us do our duty by the spirits and discuss the matter later."

So saying she led them into the room where her séances were normally conducted. Count Schulman having no choice but to follow her two other guests. The first being Cecilia de Mowbray, which might even have been her real name. A nervous and compliant lady of indeterminate age. The second guest was harder to describe. A woman shorter even than Madame Clara and yet broader, she was much given to wild yelps and utterances even when not under the influence of her spirit guide. Her name, as she gave it, being Wildflower on the basis that as a baby she had been found amongst wildflowers in the middle of a fairy ring. Had she been christened with any other name it is doubtful if even she now knew it.

This, then, was the gathering around which Madame Clara intended to perform whatever act of spiritual magic she had in mind. The exact nature of which had yet to be revealed. For the moment however, and with varying degrees of reluctance, they allowed themselves to be seated at the table, guided by the also present Nathaniel. His presence apparently necessary due to his role as confidante and protector.

Finally, almost regally, Madame Clara took her seat. Pausing for a moment until calm descended she looked around her, across the table on which no bell had been placed, to the people she would never again describe as her Camelot. This was her moment. Her time to reign supreme and claim the crown if not the throne for herself.

A long awaited opportunity, marred by the harsh croak of a raven. They were there. To guard or to warn who could say, but they had arrived unbidden and determined to make their presence known.

A yelp from Wildflower then more ravens joined in. At every window they called out; not a threat, but perhaps a warning. Harsh calls that unsettled, that moved. Answered by a scream from Cecilia de Mowbray, by more yelps from

Wildflower, the calls continued. Ravens urgently screeching to foolish mortals, telling them this was not the night to summon spirits. Too many were already abroad and who knew which of them would respond to the invitation.

Who knew indeed. Certainly not Madame Clara who nevertheless chose to ignore the warning. Thinking it only an interruption of no consequence she jumped from her chair to angrily drag shut the drapes at each of the windows.

"Begone," she screamed, her voice just as harsh.

Of this, the ravens seemingly took heed. Strangely, wondrously, their calls ceased. From that moment all was silence. A long, deep, silence broken only by one last mournful cry of a single raven before it too took flight.

Madame Clara had triumphed. Her will had prevailed, or so it seemed to her astonished guests who could only gaze at her as she stood before them, savouring her victory. Who now could say this was not to be her night.

No-one there for sure. Blissfully ignorant, they could have no idea the ravens had left of their own free will, not by any command. Their warning had been given and if mortal humans chose to ignore it there was naught else to be done. In the view of the ravens they would have to take their chances unaided against the dark forces already gathering.

Such a view was necessary because that night the ravens were needed elsewhere. As they alone knew elemental forces were appearing. Gathering in numbers, gathering in strength, they would soon be all around to the peril of any innocent souls who would soon be in need of their avian guardians, or their God.

Indeed on that fateful night, as they alone knew, the ravens were needed everywhere, as would soon be seen. The threads of this story now being weaved together are such that other events, in other places, need to be related so their significance can be understood. Their significance, true, but also their timing in regard to each other.

Accordingly, then, we must now journey across the city to a place where the ravens had least need to go. A holy place. A place of worship where the dark forces were to be fought against rather than invited in. The place where, as the reader will doubtless have guessed, was to be found Canon Jefferies.

At this time he was not in his rooms. Rather he was in the church itself, preparing his vestments for the service he was about to perform. His attempt to strike back at the devil by rescuing the precious souls of those unknown individuals who had been taken for the profit of Jacob Arthan. A holy quest indeed and one on which he intended to utilise all the power he could muster. That night his Lord, his church and his congregation would be as one.

Even as he prepared himself the part of that particular trinity which required a physical presence were already assembling. By which is meant the congregation were taking their seats and yet it has to be said as they did so troubled looks passed between them. Even they it seemed were affected by the strange air so readily apparent that evening. A tense feeling as if of a great anger simmering and rising, needing little more for it to break.

It was there throughout the city yet centred around the church which stood, rock-like, against it. As the wind howled and the dark clouds thickened the house of God stood resolute;

steadfast against whatever forces were aligned against it. In that building, alone out of all those in the city, no windows rattled nor did candles flicker. Proof indeed the storm was no mere act of nature. That evening other forces were at work; their presence clearly evident.

This was plainly visible in fact to all those in the immediate vicinity. Whether they be on their way to join the congregation or just passing by no-one could fail to notice the strange scene now being played out around them. In the middle of it: the church. With all candles lit and shining out through every window it was, as it always had been, a beacon of hope, of salvation. Yet all around it stood the darkness. Neither moon nor stars showing, the blackness was complete so that only the few who stopped to stare could see the clouds churning and broiling as if wild creatures were fighting within them. This was surely an unnatural act ... or was ungodly the right term.

"It seems perhaps the devil knows of our intentions," Canon Jefferies mused, the sullen air having penetrated the church.

A conclusion few could doubt. Certainly not Miss Burton who stood with him, fussing over his wardrobe.

Now, at his words, she paused to give him a worried look.

"Is it wise to upset the devil?" she asked.

Seeing her concern he smiled softly before saying, "To anger the devil is to please God. He will protect us from all harm."

Re-assured by this she smiled back at him, returning to her wardrobe duties for a while before asking the next question.

"And the bishop? Has he approved this?"

Here a decided twinkle could be seen in the eyes of Canon

Jefferies as he answered. "Most likely he will. Once I tell him."

His reply needing no further clarification Miss Burton merely gave him a smile as between those who had a shared secret and said nothing. Her concern in all this not being with the affairs of church, but with Doyle whose absence she had already noted. Hence her concern over angering the devil.

"What of those not here?" she murmured. "Will they too be safe?"

"You mean Doyle," the canon stopped what he was doing to look at her gently. At her nod he continued. "He is with the police who will keep him safe." After a pause he then added, "And in this he has already shown himself to be under the protection of powers far greater than they. He will come to no harm."

It was his manner, quiet and confident, rather than his words which convinced Miss Burton. Thus assured she left him to his final preparations and silent prayer while she took her place with the congregation. All of them finding peace not just in the sanctity of the building, but also in no small part from the music now being played on the organ, melodious and reverential as it was.

Comfortable and familiar, it calmed them all, even the choir who, despite being under the stern eye of the choir master, were prone to fidgeting as young boys often do. The more so as this was for them a late hour to be in the church. Their presence obtained only by special dispensation from the canon who understood the power of such innocent voices in these matters. It would be their voices above all which most called to God.

It was also their voices which called the congregation to hymn as the canon appeared; his slow procession down the aisle marked by organ and voice, rising to crescendo as he approached the altar. The power of the church indeed, and also its glory. Against this the dark forces could surely never prevail.

They were to be vanquished, cast out. At least, they would be by the church. In another part of the city, however, just as the canon was approaching the altar Madame Clara was savouring her apparent victory over the ravens. Soon too she would be holding court. The consequences of this more difficult to predict and yet of one thing there could be no doubt. For good or ill the two were now inextricably linked.

The one would decide the fate of the other.

Chapter Sixteen

The Storm Begins

Oblivious to all of these above mentioned events, Doyle and the police were meanwhile on their way to the home of Jacob Arthan. The journey hindered in some part by the wildness of the evening. More still by the irrational nature of the storm around them. At times blowing hard so that headway verged on the impossible while in between all was calm, yet not serene. The air itself heavy with a meaning few could translate.

Beyond doubt something evil was afoot; something not even the ravens could withstand. That much was clear, at least to Doyle, when they arrived at the avenue in which Jacob Arthan had his residence. Wide, tree-lined and prosperous, as it was, no doubt in the summer it was a most desirable area. Trees in bloom and far more streetlights than were to be found in the poorer quarters would have made it a place where the rich could feel both comfortable and safe.

In the bleakness of November, however, the trees were far less inviting. Gaunt and bare as they were their purpose was now only to provide an occasional perch for the ravens, wind permitting. With each gust they would be blown off the bare branches to fly high and far at the mercy of that same wind until it died away and they could return to their post. That particular tree which stood outside the door of Jacob Arthan.

Their tenacity undoubted and yet in this instance all in vain. As the storm battered forces of the law arrived they were met by a lone figure who appeared as if from nowhere. Inspector Allaby's spies, it seemed, were adept at finding hiding places.

That the lone figure was a spy belonging to the inspector was obvious beyond need of guessing. The clue being not just the way he appeared, but in the earnest conversation they were soon having.

The report was apparently not to the liking of the inspector judging by the way his face tightened at the news.

"The man has already gone," he told Doyle. "He left in a coach and horse but minutes ago."

Bad news indeed. Made worse by the fact that as Doyle stole a glance towards the ravens he saw them once again being blown helplessly by the wind. It would not do to rely on their directions this time, nor yet their protection as he had to accept.

"His destination?" he asked of the inspector only to receive a shrug.

"My men were on foot," the other replied. "He was soon lost to them."

Even more bad news and yet not the end of it surely. They had come too far just to see the man escape, of that they were determined, but what more could be done?

"Our intellect must take the place of knowledge," Inspector Allaby declared. "Where would we expect him to be going?"

"Somewhere far from here," Doyle answered, stating what

was surely obvious before looking back at the inspector. "A boat from the docks?"

This the inspector considered before shaking his head.

"Passage cannot always be arranged easily even when there is no shortage of funds," he decided. "And until the boat sailed he would be trapped."

Not an action likely of one such as Jacob Arthan, yet if the man could never be safe in that city then he must be fleeing to another, perhaps to the capital itself. Where better? Amongst that teeming metropolis he could easily lose himself before boarding a ship for the colonies or even the Americas.

Their thoughts coinciding both men knew of only one way that could be achieved. The only possible way for their quarry to make his escape. Therefore, his only possible destination.

"The railway station."

They spoke the words together, each one smiling broadly at the agreement of the other. Together, surely, they were right. He was on his way to take a train.

"And will be making poor time in this weather," the inspector declared. "If we take to the back roads we might yet catch him."

It was a hope at least. In such a fierce and unpredictable wind a coach would perforce need to travel slowly, the horse more coaxed than driven. For which reason those who used the side streets, instead of the main thoroughfares which a coach must take, might yet make up ground already lost. Perhaps not enough to catch the man on the street, but, if luck was with them, to apprehend him at the station itself.

A wild chase they knew, and one which rested solely on the

railway timetable, yet if they could be there before the train arrived they would have their man. If not then the devil did indeed look after his own. Their quarry gone forever.

So, with no-one prepared to wager on the outcome, they, nevertheless, set off with all due speed, the ravens also taking flight as they did so. To follow being impossible against such a wind they could only fly high to look down as the chase unfolded. Yet in all that it would be wrong to say they were helpless.

As they flew they called out. Long calls carried everywhere by that same wind. Impossible to be heard by those on the ground, not even by Doyle, yet still they called. Their message not meant for human ears.

It was meant for others who could hear, others who would listen. More than that they took note, they acted. Their plan unknowable to all but themselves, yet it was there. Another storytelling as a bastion against the dark for, as time would soon show, the ravens had yet a part to play in the following events. Their presence necessary, indeed vital.

*

That events were reaching a climax was becoming evident, certainly around the church. There the clouds had thickened. The air itself heavy as if fresh forces had been added to the battle, for battle it was. Good and evil ranged against each other both in the heavens and on the Earth.

Only the church itself was at peace. Inside its walls there was no trace of the turmoil taking place outside. No sign of the vast forces clearly assembled, nor of their conflict. Such things were beyond their understanding, perhaps by design, but if so was it the ineffable plan of God or the diabolic plan of Satan. To which no-one of this earth could find the answer. In this, as it ever was, mere humans were oblivious to it all.

Nevertheless, beyond the church a mighty scene unfolded. A scene only the ravens could properly appreciate as they looked down over the city to the buildings below being shaken by successive gusts of wind; its presence marked by snow flurries now being blown about, now falling silently. Truly only they could understand the cause of it all, or its import. As only they knew on the outcome of this battle rested the fate of many souls.

In the pulpit Canon Jefferies was calling on the apostles to throw out the evil spirits just as Christ had done so long ago. The gospels giving such words as the canon now repeated. Powerful words; words of mastery and command.

"Be strong in the Lord and in his mighty power," he intoned, his words taken from the scriptures. "Put on the full armour of God, so that you can take your stand against the devil's schemes. Our struggle is not against flesh and blood, but against the rulers, against the authorities, against the powers of this dark world and against the spiritual forces of evil in the heavenly realms."

Effective words. On their being said a calm came over the city. The wind died away. The snow even ceased as a long, gentle, calm began. The battle over, but what of the war.

Had defeat been admitted. Was one side in retreat, taking the storm with them, or was this merely a respite. A gathering of strength for a fresh onslaught.

The answer was soon given. Its arrival signalled not by trumpet blast, but by howling wind. Fierce and hard it blew as the battle was re-joined. Clouds swirling around the church as if it was at the very centre of a vortex. Satan, apparently, would give up nothing without a fight.

In the church, still calm, the canon had finished his sermon. The Holy Book in both hands he raised it towards the heavens as organ, then choir, then congregation began their final hymn. Voices raised against the darkness, calling to their God.

A final supplication that echoed throughout the sky itself. The wind now as of a wave crashing against harbour wall. Its power kept at bay by strong buttress. The clouds also no longer churning, but still. Throughout the heavens, it seemed, forces for good and evil were locked together. One last titanic struggle in which both were waiting for a single event to decide the outcome. A turning point to settle all of which no mortal was even aware.

Inside the church the canon certainly had no knowledge of it. His sermon over, he could have no idea more was needed, or where it would come from. Still less could he know the final outcome.

Nor could the ravens. Only God could know and God, as ever, kept his own counsel. His plans not for the understanding of mortal man as has always been the case.

Chapter Seventeen

A Darkness Not of the Night

If the church was a haven of tranquillity, on the inside at least, that could not be said of other buildings in the city. Lacking the protection afforded by being the house of God they shook with each successive blast of wind. The same wind that made their windows rattle. The same wind too that howled around them as if of wild beasts unleashed, or lost souls calling for salvation.

A wild night, then, as has already been said. A night when most folks were gathered around fire and hearth, the better for its warmth to keep the icy drafts at bay. Certainly not a night to be out of doors or visiting others and yet, in the unfolding of this tale, some were in that exact situation. The night deliberately chosen if not by them.

These were, of course, the guests of Madame Clara who were now obediently taking their seats around the table. Her apparent victory over the ravens giving her that much authority at least. Now they sat quietly, waiting on her words as the wind howled outside.

"The spirits are indeed troubled," she announced once the

storm subsided for a while. "Hear their cries."

In this there was no make believe. More than just those assembled there would swear they heard voices in the wind; sometimes crying out or others drowned by wild shrieks caused by what they dared not ask. Troublesome sounds indeed, enough to give even the bravest pause for thought, and yet Madame Clara would not be deterred.

"Come," she all but ordered, her arms spread wide. "Let us do our duty by the spirits."

The answer coming not from her guests, but by the sudden rattling of windows struck by violent gusts of wind.

They joined hands. Lamps now extinguished, the darkness all but complete, they sat in silence, each of them waiting. Soon they would begin, but first the preparation. The silence in which they would each compose themselves.

Outside the wind continued to howl, then slowly died away. A sign surely, taken as such by Madame Clara.

"Spirits we hear you," she began, her words calm and assured. "Come to us. Speak to us, through me, so we may find a way to calm you."

As if in answer the wind howled again. Its undulating cries making hands grip tightly around the table, as well they might. This was no normal storm. It held evil. Within it were sentient forces that heard Madame Clara's invitation and came to her.

Only the ravens would see it, had they been there. Only their eyes would see the darkness as it oozed through windows to pool on the floor, spreading slowly around the table. Its power growing, then held in check as the wind once more died away.

Another quiet moment into which Madame Clara spoke again.

"Spirits I beseech you. Come to us. Let me be the medium by which you reach this world so that we may aid you. In this I offer myself freely."

Words no mortal should have said in the presence of the darkness. Words that were more than just invitation. They gave it strength. They gave it permission which not even the light of God could deny.

Unknowing of this Madame Clara was forced into silence once more by the banshee shrieks of the wind. The dark forces outside once more in the ascendant. The dark forces inside now able to grow, to spread, to encircle the humans now almost in their grasp.

Still unaware of any other presence in the room they sat while all around them the shadow grew, a dark wall completely surrounding them, towering over them. Its evil almost ready to engulf them. To consume them.

Except in a different part of the city Canon Jefferies had just called on the apostles. His words reaching out even this far. As they did so the shadow convulsed as if struck by blow. Its power lost, taken from it. No longer able to sustain itself it shrank back, slowly disappearing as a long calm descended.

A silence in which could be heard the gasps of amazement from the humans who, had they known, would have considered themselves blessed. As it was, and still unknowing, they sat together, regaining their composure. All of them content merely to sit quietly in that deep tranquillity.

Eventually, and inevitably, Madame Clara roused herself.

"Spirits if you are still there have you found peace?" she asked. "Give us a sign that we may know."

Through long seconds the calm remained. Then the answer came, fierce and wild. The wind returned and with it came the darkness. Spreading out hungrily it reached for them, encircling them once more. Its presence now so powerful even they were aware of it. An oppressive evil now felt, almost seen, in the room beside them.

Quickly it built up. No longer stealthy it reared up around them, even more powerful than before. Tendrils of shadow reaching out over human heads; linking up with each other. A cage, or a net for souls.

At which point the canon raised the Holy Book aloft. His call to the Almighty, the voices of children, also calling, the congregation adding their pleas, they all combined as one. A single prayer to a single deity, who answered, who gave them a sign.

Its effect was immediate. A power invisible even to raven eyes forced the shadow back, barred it from its prey. Protected, but not yet safe the mortal humans sat immobile. Knowing naught of wider events they could only sit, frozen in fear. Still gripping hands they could only wait.

They were at a tipping point. The balance not yet decided, but beyond their power to control. Be it for good or evil they would take no further part in it.

Mortal beings as they were they could only wait for events not yet unfolded. A victory, or defeat, that would be decided elsewhere, but on which depended their very souls. Yet, despite it all, they could merely stay in their seats, frozen, helpless and completely at the mercy of others and the actions they would soon be taking. Each one unknown to the other.

As for the other parties in this tale their task was by far the hardest. Being out of doors, as they were, they were buffeted mercilessly by the wind. Their coats flapping around them. Their voices, even their very breath, snatched away it took all their effort just to stumble forward. A sorry state indeed for those involved in so desperate a chase.

As the reader will doubtless have guessed these people were in fact Doyle and the police. Their purpose that night, as the reader will also recollect, being to chase after Jacob Arthan in the hope he may be arrested. The chances of this not being very high they could only hope the storm that hindered them would equally delay him.

Both parties, therefore, in a race which only the ravens could see. Flying high as they were, and calling to each other, only they knew of the slow headway being made by both sides. Of more concern only they knew the pursuers were gaining no ground. Jacob Arthan was still ahead and more than holding his own. His escape, it seemed, was assured.

For sure there was no chance of those on foot catching him, not when they too had to battle the wind, the force they all had to struggle against which was also the deciding factor. More than that, as they were soon to discover, it was also the force that kept the contest equal. Without it there could be only one winner. In this fable the tortoise which was the police could never hope to catch the hare which was the coach and horse.

A simple fact made immediately obvious when they too experienced that long calm occasioned by the canon. In that instant the horse was able to pick up a speed no-one on foot, already tired and wind beaten, could ever hope to match. The gap between then widening as fast as the only, inescapable, conclusion could be drawn. Unknowingly, it seemed, the canon had aided villainy.

As such it certainly appeared. The coach now able to be caught by no man the villain would soon make good his escape. As he would have done, except more than just men were involved in this chase. Ravens were also there.

No longer scattered by wind they swooped low over the coach, over the horse, harsh cries making the beast start. Head turning to the left, then the right, it came to a halt, hooves pawing the ground as it stood, torn between two masters. The first wanting it to trot on, backed by whip, the second telling it to go no further. Of the two the raven call was stronger, more insistent. Yet the whip was not to be ignored.

Stern masters both the simple creature was torn between them, to its obvious discomfort. At each raven call its head swung towards the sound. At each lash of the whip its haunches bulged, forelegs straight. Again the raven call and again the whiplash, further upsetting the horse now bucking under its yoke.

Hind legs kicked out back, then front. Body heaving and head shaking it called out, its pain to be met by the same answer: raven call and whiplash. Neither permitting the other, both insisting on obedience.

Impossible to follow both commands, the horse threw its head back, calling out its agitation. Then, again struck by whip, it reared up. Hooves flying, calling out once more it tottered, it staggered. On hind legs only it pulled against its harness. The coach itself now rocking dangerously. One wheel off the ground, the other splintering under the extra weight. Soon it gave way. The coach fell on its side with a crash, dragging the horse to the ground where it lay panting, but quiet. The ravens no longer calling.

For long moments all was still. The only movement coming from a single raven landing beside the horse to stare at it through soft eyes. Gently, almost tenderly, it looked until satisfied the animal had taken no lasting hurt, after which it returned to the skies. The decision taken for it by the door of the coach being flung open and the occupant climbing out. That and the other onlookers now rushing to help, hopefully out of kindness, but possibly to remove the coach which was now an obstruction to them all.

In either way the scene was nothing but confusion. Some were being useful in helping to right the coach and bring the horse back to its feet while others, as is always the way, either shouted conflicting instructions or just stood and watched, causing their own obstruction. It was, therefore, a perfectly natural state of affairs as happens whenever there is no-one in authority present to take charge. How else to explain the fact that, despite the crowd, Jacob Arthan was able to slip away unnoticed.

Clutching just a single case, presumably full of ill-gotten money, he ran as fast as he was able, his destination still the same. Only the route varied as he was now able to make use of the same side lanes and back streets as his pursuers. Another simple fact which was to prove his undoing.

As he turned the corner from back lane into street he both saw and was seen by the police at the far end of that same street. There was still some distance between the two, the chase not yet over, but they had sight of him and that was enough. Their prayers, it seemed, had been answered.

That thought alone was enough to raise them, and they made fresh efforts, sure now of their catch. He was theirs, of that they were certain, until darker forces intervened. Once more the storm returned and it came with a vengeance. Gusts of wind to send them staggering as wild howls filled their ears and the ravens scattered. Against such a storm no-one was immune.

Their only consolation in all of this being that the same forces also affected Jacob Arthan. Even half blinded by snow and gale as they were his figure could be intermittently seen, also battling the elements. The race still even and yet under such conditions no ground could be gained. Their quarry kept his lead, and his chance of escape.

Still they fought on. Down streets now deserted they staggered, they stumbled. Sometimes losing their man, sometimes having him in plain sight. Ahead of them always, he fought through, getting ever closer to the railway station and escape. His one last obstacle being to cross the bridge.

That bridge. The bridge where so many others had been taken to their doom. The bridge of dark memory to Doyle and vigil to the canon. The bridge which harboured its own secrets.

Now in sight it stood before them, grim and foreboding. A dark shape fitfully lit only by the lights of Man yet, storm battered as it was, Jacob Arthan was still prepared to brave it. His determination to escape outweighing all other considerations he staggered forward until, unexpectedly, he need stagger no more.

Elsewhere the canon had just raised his Holy Book. His prayer answered and a sign given. A sign that reached out across the city to those battling the elements. They too felt it. They too saw its effect.

Suddenly all was calm, hushed even. A silence in which could be heard the footsteps of him running, and those chasing after him. As yet still some distance away, but catching up at a pace. The gap between them closing.

Closing, but still there so they could only watch as two uniformed constables barred his way. There to patrol the bridge as they had been instructed after agitation from church and press now, in their eyes, they could at last perform a useful function. It would be they who apprehended the criminal so clearly fleeing from those behind him. In which case the chase, surely, was over.

Rather, it would have been had the man not played one last, desperate, card. At sight of the constables he fumbled in his coat pocket to produce something those behind had no way of seeing. For that they had no guess, until they heard the pistol shot. Villain as he was the man was shooting at defenceless constables.

A second shot followed quickly as Inspector Allaby frantically waved the constables away. Their lives worth more than the capture even of so black-hearted a villain as Jacob Arthan his duty was clear. Much as it galled the man had to be let through. In the name of all humanity and decency there was no other choice.

The police scattering, the man was now free to start crossing the bridge. Those behind still chased hard, but warily. Forced not to get too close they could only follow at a distance, almost reaching the bridge themselves until the ravens took a hand. Their calls loud and urgent.

Of them all only Doyle understood. His own dark memories of that place being revived he called a halt. His companions, the police, had no knowledge of his reasons yet still they stopped. The urgency, the fear, in him unmistakeable. There, of course, because he knew why the ravens were warning them away.

Their eyes alone could see it. The darkness, rising from the river to infect the bridge with its evil. Shadows dark and thick hanging from the very beams. A great mass of it lying, pulsating, on the road. It was everywhere. A trap into which Jacob Arthan ran.

All at once it was around him, clinging to him. The bridge lit only by the lights of Man, not God, it was unstoppable. Its power far greater than the ravens. Beyond control, beyond prayer, it took hold of a mortal soul and claimed it for its own. Those watching unable to prevent it.

Indeed, those watching, excepting Doyle, were not even aware of it. They simply saw the man come to a stop, running no more. Instead, and to their confusion, they saw him turn to look out over the river, briefly to turn away. An unseen battle being fought, and soon lost. The sign of it being him turning back to the river, there to stand motionless.

Another battle not worth the fight to the mortal mind affected. No longer under his own control he stepped forward, he climbed the barrier. He stopped for only a second, two at most, then he threw himself forward. Arms outstretched, his mouth making silent scream, he launched himself into the void.

Into oblivion.

After a life lived dishonestly full of lies, of deceit and of evil in the end he also cheated the hangman. For sure no judge would be asking God to have mercy on his soul, nor did he have right of appeal. He had been taken by forces even darker than he and with as little mercy. In some ways, then, perhaps a just end.

A view which might possibly have been shared by those watching had they been so inclined. Instead, being more merciful they stood in silence; shocked and, indeed, regretful that it had come to this. A finale dictated not by justice, but by darker intent and marked by the splash of Jacob Arthan hitting the water below. His body lifeless.

Yet his soul remained, even if entrapped. As the ravens watched shadows circled over the water where the body now lay. Spinning, twisting, fighting each other like scavengers on a carcass they gathered to guard, some might say capture, the very soul of the man. The devil taking what it had always owned.

More than that it could never take, other powers were at hand to prevent that, yet not even they could stop the devil taken its own, freely given, property. So, take it the devil did. In full measure and without restraint it collected the soul of Jacob Arthan.

As it did so a change came over the entire city. Around the

church the wind ceased and clouds gradually began to disperse. Likewise, in the home of Madame Clara the shadow melted away, no longer able to threaten. As with those now walking slowly across the bridge to the fatal spot they could fell a long calm descending. The world once more at peace.

A wild night now over. One soul lost, but others gained in what some might see as a bargain well made. Certainly, at the end of it the devil took only its due.

Chapter Eighteen

The Aftermath

As is common after nights of wild storms the next day was fine and clear. The slight frost as was there served only to freshen the air and crispen the morning. A good time to be about, in short. Nature itself seeming to be making amends for the extremes of the night.

That there had been extremes was obvious from the freshly scrubbed, wind scoured streets and roofs now in need of repair. Once more the common aftermath of a storm. There was, then, nothing unusual about the day with everything perfectly normal, including that other natural result of a storm. Namely, the exceedingly low water level of the river.

To the fanciful mind it was as if the water had been swept away to make visible huge swathes of the riverbed. The general detritus of city and port now exposed. To be more exact no longer hidden by dark water, allowing it to be seen how much the river had been used as a convenient refuse pit by all and sundry.

Wooden planks, half rotted, were now in plain sight, held fast by the thick mud. Alongside these were large rocks, once the ballast of some great ship, together with corroded and stained metal plates whose original function was beyond guessing. Broken pottery and bottles were scattered about the riverbed, all colour gone, leached away by that same dark water. All in all, then, the life of the city could be read in the pages of that dark and clinging mud.

More than that the life of the river could also be read; the activities of man no longer hidden. For sure one such activity was plain to all as there, settled in the mud, lay a boat. Too pristine to have been there long it could only have been sunk recently, but by what agency had yet to be discovered.

Not that such matters bothered the mud larks who first chanced upon it. Urchins and those destitute enough to scratch a living of sorts by what could be recovered from the river. They it was who first braved the mud to climb on board, hoping to gain at least the price of a meal from whatever they might find there. So, it was they who first prised the cabin door open. They who first saw the grisly sight.

It was also their cries and alarums that drew others to the scene. Onlookers naturally for there is something in the nature of us all that will be forever attracted to calamity and deeds most foul. To more than just the common herd such things are irresistible. So it was that when the police arrived, there for reasons of duty, a crowd was already gathering; there for reasons no better than idle curiosity.

In such vein they watched as the police laid planks over the mud, the safer for them to walk on as they in turn climbed onto the boat. Its contents no longer a mystery, but requiring verification nevertheless.

For sure none but the hardiest of souls would have chosen to look into that cabin and seen the sight laid out before them. A sight of death and decay. A sight of putrefaction and the foulest of murders.

Meeting their gaze as they looked into the cabin were four human corpses. Bones protruded from the remains of flesh, teeth grinning in a clearly visible skull, this was indeed no sight for the God-fearing. Only those whose duty gave them no choice would remain in such a place, and even then not willingly. Yet stay they must for these were no accidental fatalities. Beyond doubt these deaths were at the hands of others.

A fact obvious not by inspection of the corpses, which would happen later, but by further consideration which roused the anger even of those experienced in the ways of unlawful deaths. Witnesses to the result of many a violent act they may have been, but not even they had seen anything so callous. This was murder, deliberate and cowardly. Both confirmed by the chains still shackling each and all of the bodies.

At wrist and at ankle manacles bound them fast, chains then securing them to a bolt on the floor. The arrangement serving to hold them in place so when the boat sank their fate was sealed. Beyond all help as they were when the boat sank beneath the water they were doomed to an end all sailors face, and pray to avoid. An unmarked, watery, grave.

So clear a case, and so foul an act, somewhat naturally brought more than just uniformed constabulary to the scene. Other figures also arrived whose names will be familiar. Together they gathered as, before what was now a large crowd,

216

each body was carefully carried ashore to be placed under the charge of Doctor Stanhope.

It will come as no surprise that this was also carried out under the watchful eyes of the ravens. Their arrival being silent and gradual it went unremarked by most until a goodly number had arrived. A storytelling as the canon described it, everyone else seeing them as an unkindness, seekers of calamity. The exception being Doyle who looked at the crowds now assembled and wondered how they were any different from their opinion of the ravens. Both being there to witness the same, inhuman, sight.

A thought taken further by the consideration that the ravens had earned the right to be there although that he kept to himself as Inspector Allaby neared him.

"So now we know," he announced, his face grim set. "That can only be the boat sunk by Joseph Malloy."

At this Doyle nodded. "I remember when Sergeant Walters told the story of that night he said the rattling of chains could be heard, and sounds they thought came from animals."

"When instead it was those poor wretches," the inspector muttered with a nod towards the shrouded corpses being carried away. "Little wonder no-one would reveal what contraband was being carried that night."

Here also Doyle could only agree. In the eyes of those members of the gang as had been caught it was obviously better to let the police assume it was liquor and tobacco being carried. Admitting it was more lost souls eventually to be sold to the medical profession would have gained them far harsher treatment, not to mention the noose. Reason enough for their silence.

Cause also for Doyle and the inspector to fall equally silent as they contemplated the affair. Eventually, after no more than a minute or two, the inspector stirred.

"I heard that when Arthan's country house was entered a sword was found. The murder weapon most likely," he told Doyle.

Doyle nodded in response to this final puzzle piece revealing itself.

"So, all in all, a satisfactory ending for your story."

This, of course, being so true Doyle could only agree with a smile not wholly out of place in such grim surroundings. It was indeed a satisfactory ending to what he knew would be a well-received story. The kind more than one magazine would vie to serialise before the novelette itself was published. Its success, therefore, was assured as was some slight fortune he could expect to earn from it. By his calculation more than sufficient for a man of good standing to contemplate marriage.

In his eyes, then, a very satisfactory conclusion. The same could be said for Inspector Allaby. Not only had he solved his crime so that the chief perpetrator would at least face the judgement of God if not Man, but he could also look forward to a favourable commentary in the soon to be published story of it all. Of that he was assured by the look which passed between himself and Doyle, the one telling the other the debt would be paid. His reputation would only be enhanced when the story was told.

A satisfactory ending for all then. Enough to put the

inspector in some quite good humour as he was called away to deal with matters requiring the authority of his rank. In this case regarding the eventual disposal of the corpses.

"More examples for the pathology?" he asked of Doctor Stanhope who was standing beside them, almost as if on guard.

At this question the doctor gave a sigh, shaking his head as he did so. "Not this time," he answered slowly as if tired of the entire business, and what it had come to. "Let the church have them," he continued in the same vein before turning to look at the inspector. "The medical profession can wait."

Another satisfactory ending to the mind of Inspector Allaby who was still careful not to let it show. It would not do to let the doctor think he was criticising the members of his profession. Instead, as befitted the occasion, he merely stood in quiet consideration beside the man.

As for Doyle he stood alone for a moment, contemplating his future, then walked the few steps to where Canon Jefferies was standing by himself.

"We have our answer," the canon told him softly as he approached.

Doyle looking confused at this the canon explained further, gesturing towards the boat as he did so.

"Those poor unfortunates, knowing they were beyond hope, must have called down their curses on all those responsible. Doing that in such dire extremity would have been enough to invite the devil into this world, and once here, evil would remain. It's foulness tethered by those agonised souls who called it."

"And now?"

"Now? Once their mortal remains are interred and their souls put to rest, Satan will be banished from here."

He paused there, the nod of his head and his smile betraying satisfaction.

"By the grace of God we have done it," he announced slowly. "Between us we have beaten the devil."

"Have we?" Doyle asked softly at which the canon gave a rueful smile.

"In truth we have only beaten the evil of man," he answered with a sigh. "The rest we may safely leave to our Lord. Our part in this is now over."

As indeed it was. The proof of it being before their gaze where, as they watched, the ravens silently took flight. No longer deeming it necessary to stay they left for places and for reasons only they could know.

Their storytelling now complete.